I0661557

Mary Elizabeth Braddon

The Story of Barbara
Her Splendid Misery and Her Gilded Cage. Vol. 3

ISBN/EAN: 9783337050085

Printed in Europe, USA, Canada, Australia, Japan

Cover: Foto ©Andreas Hilbeck / pixelio.de

More available books at **www.hansebooks.com**

Mary Elizabeth Braddon

The Story of Barbara

Her Splendid Misery and Her Gilded Cage. Vol. 3

BARBARA

LONDON :
ROBSON AND SONS, PRINTERS, PANCRAS ROAD, N.W.

THE STORY OF

BARBARA;

HER SPLENDID MISERY, AND HER GILDED CAGE

A Novel

BY THE AUTHOR OF

'LADY AUDLEY'S SECRET,' 'VIXEN,'
ETC.

IN THREE VOLUMES
VOL. III.

LONDON
JOHN AND ROBERT MAXWELL
MILTON HOUSE, SHOE LANE, FLEET STREET

[All Rights reserved]

CONTENTS OF VOL. III.

Digitized by the Internet Archive
in 2009 with funding from
University of Illinois Urbana-Champaign

BARBARA

———

CHAPTER I.

FLOSSIE ADMITS HER GUILT.

MRS. TREVORNOCK and Flossie were quick to respond
to Barbara's summons.

The little house in South-lane was a very pleasant abode in these latter days, when there was
always a certainty of sending the tax-gatherer away
rejoicing, and Amelia could have butcher's meat as
often as the most pampered footman on Denmark-
hill, were she so inclined. Friendly tea-drinkings
occasionally enlivened the monotony of domestic
life; and once in a way Mrs. Trevornock would indulge her daughter with a visit to a West-end
theatre. Their circle of friends widened a little, for
Mrs. Trevornock, with a daughter married to a

VOL. III. B

wealthy Cornish squire, and a new carpet in her drawing-room, took higher rank than of old among her acquaintance, and was asked to more stately tea-parties.

Flossie was admired, and it was prophesied by friendly matrons that she too would make a brilliant marriage in due time; she might not, perhaps, enrol herself among the landed gentry; but there were wealthy drysalters and millionaire soap-boilers floating on the surface of Camberwell society, and who could tell when one of these might be drawn into Flossie's net?

'And then she must have such opportunities at her sister's country seat,' observed the matrons; whereon Mrs. Trevornock was fain to confess that Penruth Place was like heaven, insomuch as there was neither marrying nor giving in marriage there.

But, dull as the old Cornish mansion was, the mother was always delighted to go there, and Flossie rejoiced at the variety of dulness, which gave Camberwell—and the shops in the Walworth-road—a new zest when she went back.

'And so Miss Penruth is at home, and we are to be honoured with her exhilarating society this time, are we?' said Flossie, when she had opened her box and shown Barbara her new garments, which were of the latest Paris fashion, as interpreted by a Camberwell dressmaker.

'Yes, dear, and I hope you will be polite to her.'

'Polite! I will be as elaborately civil as a character in an old comedy, "Madam, you are vastly obliging;" "I protest, madam, you overwhelm me with your undeserved condescension." Will that kind of thing please her, do you think, Bab?'

'Don't talk nonsense, Flossie. Be as polite as you can; and if she should say anything disagreeable, hold your tongue.'

'That is just the one thing I cannot do,' protested Flossie. 'If she gird at me I must gird again, though I were to risk being forbidden her brother's house for ever after.'

'Flossie, I want to ask you a serious question,' said Barbara.

It was the night of Flossie's arrival. The visitors had dined and refreshed themselves, and now it was bedtime, and the sisters were standing side by side in front of the fire in Flossie's room.

' O !' said Flossie, looking nervous.

' Major Leland is in England.'

' I should call that a statement, and not a question,' said Flossie, trying to be flippant, but inwardly disturbed.

' He is in Cornwall. I have seen him.'

' O,' said Flossie, ' I hope he is very well, and that he—enjoyed himself—in India.'

' Flossie, where did you post that letter I gave you the day I was ill, the last letter I ever wrote to Captain Leland ?'

Flossie gasped, and turned pale.

' Where did I post it ? I — well, I suppose it must have been at the watchmaker's, where the man was always so civil, you know. He's a German—or perhaps a Swiss, as he's connected with watches. The people in Switzerland seem to devote all their energies to making watches, and taking the bread out of the mouths of the people in Coventry.'

'The letter never reached him, Flossie. Our fate, his and mine, depended upon that one little letter, and he never received it.'

'I suppose if he had got the letter you and he would have been married?' asked Flossie.

'Yes.'

'Then what a blessing that he didn't get it! Think of the difference in your position as mistress of this house, and as an East India Company's Major's wife! For you know, Bab, it was all very well while he was sending in strawberries and salmon and things, we could afford to blind ourselves to the truth; but the Company's service does not rank as high as the Queen's. I'm sure, if the letter did go astray, you ought to be very grateful to Providence for that lucky accident.'

'Yes,' said Barbara bitterly, 'it has made a wide difference in my life. As George's wife I should have been happy.'

'If you are not happy in a house that was built in the time of Cromwell, you have neither artistic taste nor gratitude to God for His mercies,' said Flossie, with a religious air. 'And then think how comfortable you have been able to make poor over-worked ma. A Company's officer could not have given you six hundred a year.'

'Well, there is consolation in that ; and Vyvyan is very good to me. Do not think that I am un-grateful to him, or to Providence. But I want to know about that letter. I cannot understand why that one letter, on which so much depended, should have gone astray. Are you quite sure you posted it, Flossie ?'

'I'm quite sure I didn't,' cried Flossie, falling on her knees and bursting into tears. 'I cannot be such a horrid little story-teller as to say I did. I lost the letter, Bab dearest ; and ma and I put our heads together in the kitchen, and we both felt that it was much better for you that the letter had not gone, though there was no knowing whether some officious person in the street wouldn't pick it up and post it ; and we determined to say nothing to you about it ; and the consequence is that you are the wife of one of the richest men in Cornwall, and ought to be as happy as the days are long.'

'O Flossie, you have done your best to break two

hearts!' cried Barbara, covering her pale indignant face with her clasped hands. 'And my mother knew of this, my mother joined in the plot against me, my **mother** whom I have loved so dearly!'

'And you were in duty bound to love her,' argued the indomitable Flossie, who had dried her tears, and prepared herself for action. 'Think how unselfish **she has been; how she has always sacrificed her own** pleasure and her own comfort for ours; how she has waited upon us and cherished us, and has been father and mother both to us. Is it a great thing even if you have sacrificed your own happiness, or what you think would have been your own happiness, **in order** to make her declining years free from care? **I am** sure I would have married the vulgarest **soap-boiler** in Camberwell, a creature who only aspirates by accident, if by such a marriage I could have secured **comfort for my mother.'**

'You are right, perhaps. **I** ought to be grateful for your carelessnes and your want of candour,' Barbara answered bitterly. 'But **I** know George Leland **would not have let my** mother starve. She **would have been** cared for, God bless her!'

'I suppose you would have sent ma a ten-pound note once in a blue moon, and would have called that helping your family!' ejaculated Flossie contemptuously.

'Good-night,' said Barbara coldly; and so she left the delinquent, who knew not whether to consider herself forgiven.

Mark felt his life hedged round with danger after Flossie's arrival at Place. Molly had taken it into her head to be jealous of that young lady; and as there were eyes to see and tongues to report to her all that went on in the house, Mark felt as if he were for ever under observation. And Flossie, having no one else of the male sex to amuse her, took it into her head to be particularly fascinating to Mark, especially as she wanted to ride one of his horses.

Mark's stud had been severely reduced to two— the useful Pepper, and a thick-set brown cob, impossible for a lady to ride, and not too possible for a gentleman.

Flossie's indoor amusements at Place were

limited to novel-reading, fancy work, playing with
Mark's dogs, and eating clotted cream in every possible form. Even these mild enjoyments were
made less enjoyable by the presence of Miss Penruth, whose countenance since the young lady's
coming had fixed itself in a stony disapprobation.
Flossie's invention was exercised in finding corners
where Priscilla's severe gray eye could not reach
her. She would sit on the carpet in the embrasure
of a window, screened from view by a curtain that
smelt of bygone centuries, gloating over Currer
Bell or Mrs. Marsh; and would emerge from her
retreat at the sound of the luncheon-bell, smiling
defiance at the offended spinster, who had been
wondering where she was all the morning.

Out of doors Flossie was free as air. She
made friends with all the bipeds and quadrupeds
in the stable. She drove Barbara's ponies, with a
delightful ignorance of the first principles of driving;
and it was only the innate virtue and discretion
of those two amiable Norwegians and the primeval
solitude of the roads that saved her from ruin and
death. Mrs. Trevornock sat by her daughter's

side in happy unconsciousness of danger, and admired Flossie's skill and style on the driving-
box.

'You really are a very clever girl,' she would
say mildly. 'It seems to come natural to you to do
things right.'

'That shows the advantage of not having all
one's talent ground out of one by a schoolmistress,
ma. I really ought to be thankful to Mr. T. for never
having expended sixpence on my education.   I
daresay if I had been carefully trained at an ex-
pensive boarding-school, I should be as common-
place as other girls.'

Flossie took to horsemanship just as she took
to driving. She was utterly fearless, and she
possessed a talent for sticking to her saddle. Beyond this her gifts were small; but Mark admired
her boldness and her firm seat, and consented to
lend her even the illustrious gray Pepper, a horse
out of which he expected to make money before he
had done with him. On Pepper, Flossie scoured
the moor far and wide, sometimes attended by a
groom on one of Vyvyan's horses, sometimes alone.

She had serious thoughts of climbing Brown Willy. She could **not** ascertain that the feat had ever been **performed by** an equestrian, **and this made** the idea **so** much **the more** attractive.

CHAPTER II.

ROCKPORT is one of those places which might have been left out of the world without making much difference in the history of mankind; and yet there are few finer or bolder bits of coast scenery upon the rugged western point of England. It is not so grand a spot as the Land's End, nor so lovely as that pinnacle of many-coloured rock crowned with the Logan Stone, nor so striking as the Lizard; but the green hills and gray rocks of that quiet bay, the steep village street, the background of mountain and moor, the winding roads between ferny banks by which the stranger descends from the great Gorse Moors to the little harbour by the water's edge, the parish church among green fields, the cottages and gardens perched anyhow on the edge of a rugged hill-side,—all these are as picturesque and as interesting as anything to be found in Cornwall or in Brittany.

Here, at the cosy inn, kept by kindly people, and

running over with the fatness of the land, Major
Leland found a halting-place of most exquisite repose,
after the troubled days of the year that was gone.
He had come back to England seriously ill—come
back, as he thought, to die; and it seemed to him as
if it could matter very little to any one, not even to
Vyvyan Penruth, where he spent the last few weeks
of his life.

'I don't want to make the husband uncomfortable,' he said to himself; 'but for me it is a kind of
happiness to know that I am near the woman I shall
love till my heart ceases to beat.'

The quiet beauty of the place and its surroundings pleased him. He was just able to climb to the
topmost green point above the sea, and to lie and
rest there, smoking his cigar, watching the waves
roll in and the gulls skimming whitely above the
white crest of lead-coloured water, idly thinking of
summer nights more than a year ago, when he had
stood on the ridge at Delhi, under the purple Indian
sky and the big bright stars, watching the glancing
lights in the accursed city, where the old king and
his favourites were holding their revels in the palace

of the Great Mogul, the Centre of the Universe, the
Shadow of God on Earth, in the hall on whose walls
the boastful conqueror had inscribed, 'If there is a
paradise upon earth, it is here.' The day soon came
when the Shadow of God on Earth sat upon an old
charpoy, or four-legged bedstead, in that splendid
hall where the peacock throne once shed its rainbow
light, to be tried for his life by the power he had defied and outraged, and to be sent thence to finish the
remnant of his days as a convict in the Andamans.

Sometimes the mornings were fair and sunny,
and the sea took its summer hues of emerald and
amethyst, and a mistaken bee came humming across
the flowerless thyme in search of a belated harebell
or the last tuft of clover. Vessels passed and vanished on the distant horizon ; but they carried no
thought of George Leland with them. He felt as if
he had done with all the earth except just this lonely
corner of his native island. He spent many a tran-
quil hour in the old churchyard on the hill, and it
was sweetly sad to him to think that he might lie
there before very long, and that Barbara might come
some day and kneel beside his grave.

His sisters would gladly have had him among them in Somersetshire, where three out of the four were prosperously settled, and where he would have **been nursed and** petted exceedingly; but he shrank from the very thought of that loving circle. He wanted to be alone with his grief, now that the busy work of life was over—such work as he had done in India, which had left him so little leisure for thought.

Years had gone since the parting on board the Hesper, yet the girl he had clasped in his arms that day was no less dear to him. He had surrendered her of his own accord, believing that to do so was his duty, and he had loved her so much the more because of that surrender. Never had she been dearer to **him** than when he wrote the letter that renounced **her.** Never had she been lovelier in his eyes than **on** that day when he saw her again in her matronly pride and dignity, bearing herself calmly and nobly, true and faithful to her loveless marriage-bond.

He had no thought of seeking a second interview, of introducing himself to her husband. She had said that they might meet as friends, that nothing

forbade them to be friends; but his stronger soul
revolted against such a mockery of friendship.

'She must be all the world to me, or nothing,'
he told himself.

No one at the Waterloo Inn, Rockport, knew that
he had any acquaintance with the family at Place.
He was only known to his landlord and landlady as
an Indian officer who had come to mend a broken
constitution on that breezy coast. He soon won the
liking of host and hostess, and, the inn being almost
empty at this time of year, they devoted themselves
to making him comfortable. From his landlady,
who was inclined to indulge herself now and then
with a cheerful gossip, Major Leland contrived to
hear a good deal about Barbara and the family at
Place. He heard how good she was, how the servants liked and respected her, how kind she had
been, in her quiet unpretentious way, to the poor.

'Miss Penruth used to set herself up as the
Lady Bountiful to all the district,' said Mrs. Thomas
of the Waterloo; 'but Mrs. Penruth gives a sovereign where her sister-in-law would give sixpence,
and makes no fuss about it. And everybody knows

what a good wife she is, though nobody can suppose that she married the Squire for love.'

'So long as she is happy, that is enough,' said **George Leland.**

She had told him she was happy, and he had not believed her. He had regarded that assertion as **an** heroic falsehood.

Mrs. Thomas expatiated upon the family at Place: **she** spoke of Mr. **Mark, who** was not thought highly of, though he was liked for his easy good-nature **and** absence of pride, and who was supposed to have entangled himself in an uncomfortable **manner with** a handsome barmaid at Camelot. **And then Mrs.** Thomas told her lodger all she could tell about the cottage on the St. Columb road, and how that abode **was** now shut up; whereby it was supposed that **the** Squire's brother and the barmaid had **parted;** perhaps because of the Squire having got **wind of the** disreputable alliance.

'He's just the sort of man to be very strict in such matters,' **said** Mrs. Thomas. 'The Penruths always were a proud family, all except Mark.'

She told her lodger how changed the Squire had

been by his late illness; how he had been gradually giving up all his old ways ever since last summer; and how it was supposed in the neighbourhood that he was breaking up, and would never be again the man he had been.

'They're not a long-lived family,' she remarked conclusively. 'The father was under fifty when he was taken off sudden by heart-disease. I never saw such a change in any one as in Mr. Penruth, when I saw him at church four Sundays ago. There was a strange preacher come from Plymouth to preach for the schools, and the Squire and his ladies drove over to hear him. He looked a good ten years older than he did last Christmas. He used to be the hardest rider in these parts. He'd come tearing over the moor on a big brown horse, or driving a high dog-cart, and going faster than the mail. He used to be out and about all day long. And now they d' say he sits staring at the fire or reading his newspaper for hours at a stretch. It's not his young wife's fault if he's dull and melancholy; for everybody says how good and dutiful she has been to him, though it can hardly be expected that a handsome young woman can care much for a grumpy **old man** like Vyvyan Penruth.'

'Handsome is as handsome does,' said Major Leland. 'She may have learnt to love him for the **sake** of his goodness to her. She seems happy, does she not?'

'She behaves herself as a lady should,' replied Mrs. Thomas, with a sententious air; 'everybody says that of her; and that's as much as anybody has a right to know. We can't go prying into the insides of people's hearts and minds, you see, **sir.** We must form our judgment from the outside, and be content. We've no more to do with what lies behind than we have to grumble because **there's a** dark side to the moon while her bright side is lighting us over the moor.'

Was she happy? That was the question which George Leland perpetually asked of himself? She **had assured him that all** was well with her, **that** she was happy in **her** married life. But **this** assurance he took to be a noble falsehood, a woman's sacrifice to her own self-respect. The thought that **she could** be happy **while** he was so miserable for the loss of her maddened him. He knew that this impotent jealousy, this rage against the fate that had parted them, was a base and a hateful feeling, yet he could not conquer it. He who had fought so stoutly against his country's foes was in this no hero. He could not subjugate self.

He was lying one day on a grassy headland, listless, low-spirited, having read all the news that interested him in yesterday's *Times*, and having nothing to do for the live-long day but watch the sea and the gulls, with faint hopes of an occasional cormorant to diversify the scene. The morning was mild and sunny, though November had begun; summery-looking clouds were floating in a blue sky, and lending their varied colour to a summery sea. The soft air seemed laden with a ghostly perfume, the odour of the dead year's flowers; or perhaps it was only the sweet scent of an upland turnip-field, or that untraceable mysterious perfume which exhales from the very earth on such a morning, the spirit of fallow field and fading woodland, faint breathings from hidden violets under ragged hedges where the sturdy redbreast swings a-top of a thorn, and carols his welcome to the coming winter.

Startled from a gloomy reverie, George Leland looked up at the sound of horse's hoofs bounding over the short turf, and beheld a young lady in a blue habit, fair-haired, rosy-cheeked, blue-eyed, a bright familiar face, which he had known in the happiest period of his life.

' Flossie !' he cried, starting to his feet.

'How do you do, Captain—I beg your pardon, Major—Leland ?' said Flossie, just as coolly as if they had parted yesterday.

There she sat, looking down upon him from the altitude of a big gray horse—a horse of undecided temperament, who had hardly made up his mind whether he would be gray or roan, and had subsided into a speckly mixture of both, which justified his name, Pepper and Salt. She sat her big awkward horse as easily as if she had been born in the saddle, and she was as pretty and almost as pert as she had been five years ago in the garden at Camberwell, when they two had waltzed together on the soft springy turf, amidst night dews and roses, under a summer moon. Yet at sight of his **gaunt wasted figure and faded face**, lit by large haggard **eyes, even Flossie's impertinence** was put to the **blush.**

She looked at him earnestly, her eyes filling with tears.

'You are sadly altered,' she said, 'since—since—'

'Since the happy time when we were all young; since the summer day when Barbara and I lost ourselves under the Greenwich elms. **Yes, I** daresay **I am changed since then. Such a campaign as I have gone through is not calculated to** improve a man's personal appearance.'

He spoke lightly, but his hand trembled a little as he held Flossie's **bridle, while the fidgety Pepper** dug holes in the turf with his fore-feet.

'I wish I **could hook this horse on to** something, and dismount,' **said** Flossie. 'He is a wretched **beast that** will never consent to stand still; and I **should like to have a long talk with you.'**

'I'll take care of **the** horse,' said Major **Leland;** whereupon Flossie dropped lightly from her saddle, and gave the Major **the** bridle.

There was a nondescript little building surrounded **with rusty iron** railings on the highest pinnacle of the cliff. Only a native of the soil could have told if there was any use or any intention in it. It might have been intended as a rude temple dedicated to the winds, and it might have been **that** Boreas and his brotherhood did not deem the fane worthy of **their** acceptance; for they rushed in at **its** grated windows, and tore round it and howled **over** it with exceeding savagery in tempestuous weather, **as if they had marked it for** destruction. No visitor **to Rockport** had the faintest idea of its **meaning;** but it was a mark in the landscape for those aspiring climbers who are always shouting 'Excelsior!' and the railings were handy to lean against when **one** had struggled to the summit of the grassy hill, and, **if the winds were** battering against **three** sides of the building, there **was** a chance of shelter on the fourth.

Here, the day being quiet and fair, Major Leland led the submissive Pepper, who seemed to think **he** was going to get a bait, **and** anon fastened his bridle securely to the railings on the landward side, and left the patient beast to crop the short salt turf, while he went back to Flossie, who was walking slowly up and down a narrow path upon the steep grassy slope fronting the sea. He held out both his hands and grasped hers warmly.

'I am very glad to see you, Flossie,' he said. 'There is only one other person in the world whom I would rather see.'

'You would not say that if you knew everything,' she protested, shaking her head with a contrite air; 'you would hate me.'

'I should hate you if I knew—what?'

'You are very sorry to have lost Barbara, I am afraid?' she said, looking at him deprecatingly.

'Sorry? Yes, I am sorry. It is a sorrow that will last me for my lifetime, and go down with me to my grave.'

'Don't,' cried Flossie; 'you make me feel like a murderer. Is it that sorrow which has altered you so?'

'No, my dear. Grief and regret have gnawed my heart; but I went on living all the same—ate, drank, slept, thrived as a brute thrives in his pasture. Hardship and privation, forced marches, deadly heat and dreary rain,—these are the things that have sapped my strength, and perhaps shortened my life. But, for God's sake, tell me what you mean, Flossie! Why should I hate you? what had you to do with my sorrow?'

'Ever so much. Barbara wrote you a letter.'

'Yes.'

'One very enormously particular letter.'

'Yes, I know, and it never reached me. She told me of it.'

'I lost it,' said Flossie, blurting out her confession, and looking him full in the face, with an air half deprecating, half defiant, almost as if she expected him to knock her down. 'I lost it. I had ever so many things to get for ma, and there were all kinds of new things in the shop-windows in the Walworth-road—gloves at a shilling and elevenpence-halfpenny, with the elevenpence-halfpenny written in pencil, you know—so deceiving; and there were bonnets and all sorts of fancy articles, which you wouldn't understand if I were to tell you about them; and altogether I never saw the Road more attractive; and so—I suppose I must have dropped the letter,' said Flossie very slowly, after rattling on at the rate of an express train; 'for when I got to the post-office—the watchmaker's, you know, where the man was always civil—it was gone. I don't suppose my pocket had been picked; for, you see, a thief would hardly care about a flimsy Indian letter without a stamp on it, and I had the shilling ready to pay for the stamp. That reminds me, by the bye, I owe Barbara that shilling.'

'But there was no crime in losing the letter; Barbara could have written another. Why, in Heaven's name, could you not act frankly and tell her? I thought you were all truthfulness.'

'So I am,' protested Flossie. 'My every-day character is frank to a fault. But this was one of those extraordinary events in life where one is tempted to go a little off the straight track. Don't you remember telling us about Clive—how he took in that poor old Indian with a sham treaty? and I have no doubt that, in a common way, Clive was a very frank man—'

'Never mind Clive, Flossie. Tell me why you acted so falsely.'

'Well, you see, mamma and I talked it over, and it did seem such a pity that Barbara should be engaged to you, who were thousands of miles away, and had got yourself into difficulties, when here was Mr. Penruth on the spot, and one of the richest men in Cornwall, and desperately in love with her—in love to such a degree that hothouse grapes at half a guinea a pound were as nothing to him. And mamma thought it was Providence that had interfered to make me lose that letter; and it really looked like it, for I never did such a thing before; and it would have seemed like flying in the face of Providence to go and tell Barbara, and let her write again. It would have been, as it were, frustrating the good intentions of higher powers; so we decided to say nothing to Barbara—and—that's all.'

'That's all!' echoed Major Leland. 'You only broke two hearts, or one at least. I will answer nothing for the other.'

'Come now, you said just now that it was the climate and hardships and forced marches—'

'Yes, those brought me to the brink of the grave. But it was not climate or hardship that broke my heart, Flossie. Well, I have no right to complain—I will not complain, if she is content; but to have been so near happiness and to have missed it—that is hard. At that time, when my honour and honesty had been doubted, it seemed to me my duty to release my dearest girl from her promise. To do less would have been to prove myself unworthy of her love. Was she, in her trusting faith, loving me fondly and blindly, to link her young life to a man of blighted character? The idea of such a sacrifice was intolerable to me, and I did not hesitate in writing the letter which renounced all hope of happiness. But when that lettter had gone, when the long slow months wore on, I doing journeyman's work at an up-country station, how I hungered and thirsted for a letter from my love—one little letter, telling me that she was sorry for me, that she did not let me go without regret!'

'And all that time some nasty selfish creature was treasuring up Bab's letter as a curiosity, I daresay,' said Flossie, glad to transfer some part of the burden of wrong to an unknown individual.

'I will try to be content, and think that all things have happened for the best,' said George Leland, with a smile that moved Flossie more than even tears could have done.

'We were very, very poor when Bab consented to marry Mr. Penruth,' pursued Flossie apologetically. 'Our dear mother was ill; her health seemed to be breaking up altogether. We had no one to help us. It was like the old song Barbara used to sing in those happy summer evenings. Yes, indeed, it was just the story of Auld Robin Gray over again. And now Barbara has a grand old house and a carriage and a pony-phaeton, and might wallow in gold if she liked; and poor ma and I are provided for. You would hardly know us at Camberwell. The drawing-room is lovely—new carpet, new curtains, old china—you know how clever mamma is in picking up cups and saucers and things in odd out-of-the-way brokers' shops. It is the dearest little room. We are even thinking of a new piano.'

'Can I grudge you your happiness, Flossie, even

if it has cost me my own? No, dear, I am resigned, if Barbara is happy.'

'If she is not she ought to be,' answered Flossie confidently. 'She has an excellent and most indulgent husband in his own grumpy way. She is allowed to have us for a long visit every year, and you must admit that is a privilege.'

'She has her mother with her sometimes; I am glad of that.'

'And ME,' said Flossie.

'Well, I will believe that she is happy, and be content. The greatest happiness for the greatest number, that is the supreme good. Somebody must be left out in the cold.'

'I am sure we have all reason to be thankful,' said Flossie. 'If you had come home before the Mutiny, and had married Barbara, and taken her back to India with you, think how dreadful that might have been!'

'Might have been!' echoed George Leland shudderingly. 'Yes, that would have been too horrible. My darling, my innocent dove, at the mercy of those savages! No, I thank God for the fate that parted us, if by that alone she could be saved from being even a witness **of the things** that were done by those hell-hounds! Can the few who were saved ever forget those days? Those days of anguish and suspense, when the men who were fighting for their country trembled at the thought of their dear ones far away in the hills; when every day brought its **tale of** another revolted regiment, another cruel slaughter, helpless women starving in the jungle, or hiding in cellars, danger and death in every hideous shape. Can the mothers whose babies were slain upon their breasts ever be happy again? Yes, there is something to be thankful for in that. She might **have been** amongst those forlorn ones.'

They paced slowly along the narrow track **in** silence for a few minutes, George Leland's thoughts travelling back to the year that was gone and the things that he had seen. **How** deeply he had pitied **the men** who had wives and children in those days!

'You see,' said Flossie cheerfully, after this pause, 'Providence is always good. Providence brought Mr. Penruth just when our poor mother could not have struggled on any longer without substantial help. Providence made me lose that letter.'

'And Providence brought you here this morning, I suppose, to tell me how you contrived to do it?' said the Major, with his half-sad, half-bitter smile.

'Well, I hardly know,' replied Flossie musingly. 'I had a sort of idea that I should see you if I rode this way; and as I do just as I like and go just where I like in this wild out-of-the-way hole, and have the run of that horse Pepper, which belongs to my sister's brother-in-law, Mark Penruth, a very obliging person, I thought I might just as well come and look you up.'

'You knew I was staying here?'

'Of course. Do you for a moment suppose that anybody can go anywhere or do anything in this desolate place without everybody else knowing all about it?'

'Did Barbara know you were coming?'

'O dear, no! I didn't so much as hint at my intention. She might have asked me not to come.'

'And will you tell her that you have seen me?'

'I think not. It couldn't do any good, you

know, and it might **unsettle her mind.** The very **best thing she can do is to forget your existence, which, by** the way, she can hardly be expected **to do** while you are living within half a dozen miles of her **house.** Don't you think you **could** contrive to go and get well somewhere else?'

'I shall not stay here much longer. **But I like** the quiet of the place, **and the air has** done wonders **for me.'**

'Poor fellow! How **bad** you must have been **before** you began to get better!' exclaimed Flossie, **with a** compassionate look at his hollow cheeks.

'Yes, I shall soon move on upon my journey, Flossie. **It matters** very little where **I go for the** rest—'

'For the rest of your furlough, **or** whatever you call it,' interrupted Flossie. '**If you are** indifferent where **you go,** why shouldn't **you come** and stay with **us at** Camberwell, **when we go** back, which is to be in a week or two? Mamma would be delighted to **have you**—as a visitor, you know; **and she and I** would take such **care of you, and** feed you up **till** you were as strong as **a** lion. Ma makes delicious beef-tea and jelly and all the things an invalid ought to have. Do come.'

'You are very good, Flossie. Yes, I should like to be under your roof; there would be sadness in it, but pleasure too—to walk up and down the old garden-path where she and I dawdled away so many an hour. But I should hardly recognise your house and garden in winter. When I call up the picture of that garden it is always summer, summer evening, and Venus is shining placidly in the pale-gray sky above the hazels at the end of the walk, and the soft air is scented with roses and jasmines. Yes, I should dearly like to be in your quiet little home, Flossie. It is a happy thought of yours. There is no place that would do me so much good.'

'I am so glad,' faltered Flossie. 'I will do all I can to please you and to make up for my careless-ness, for my wickedness, about that letter. And now I must go back as fast as I can. Poor Pepper must be tired of those railings, and I'm afraid he will have eaten enough grass to make himself ill.'

'Hardly, I think, with the bit in his mouth. And now, Flossie, one word before we part. If it should ever come **to your** knowledge **that** your sister **were in any trouble of mind,** any difficulty, in which a man's honest will could aid her, remember that **I** would **give** my life **to** save her an hour's **pain.** Remember, dear, though I shall love her fondly to the end of all things, I am a soldier and a gentleman, and I am to be trusted. It is not likely that she will ever need my help, but God knows it would be given faithfully.'

'I am sure of that,' said Flossie, as they walked up the slope to the railed enclosure. 'And it is a promise that you are to come to us, is it not?'

'Yes, it is a promise.'

'I shall write to you here when I know the date of our return.'

'Could you not ride over and see me again?'

'Do you really like to see me?'

'Very much.'

'**Then I'll** come.'

And presently she was mounted on Pepper, and rode slowly off, smiling back at the Major, as she walked her horse zigzag fashion down the breast of **the hill.**

CHAPTER III.

A FRIENDLY WARNING.

SOME days passed before Mark could find any opportunity for private conversation with the inestimable Mrs. Morris. That lady's caution was so great that she avoided all encounters with the Squire's brother which might possibly come within the ken of any member of the household. But after that interview with his brother, in which Vyvyan had revealed the contents of his will, Mark had a natural desire to impart his knowledge to the woman whom it concerned so nearly. He watched his opportunity therefore, and came home earlier than usual from the quarries one afternoon at the beginning of November, in order to lie in wait for Mrs. Morris in the dusky corridor, before the lighting of lamps and candles.

He had not been long in the corridor, lounging on a window-seat, looking absently out at the shadowy hills, when Mrs. Morris appeared, carrying the afternoon letters and papers on a salver. Miss Penruth excelled as a letter-writer, and kept up a wide correspondence with absent friends. What they could all find to write about must ever remain a mystery to the outside world.

At sight of Mark's figure, half hidden by the embrasure of the window, Molly started and paled. She had seemed curiously nervous of late—the effect, perhaps, of her false position, which must trouble even so skilled a dissimulator.

'Take the letters,' said Mark, 'and then come back to me as quick as you can. I want a talk with you.'

She nodded yes, and tripped lightly away with her salver; and in three minutes came back to him, and seated herself quietly by his side in the dusk.

It was the servants' tea-time, the hour for buttered toast and unlimited gossip, and there was little chance of any one coming to light the lamps yet awhile.

'What is it all about, Mark?' she asked.

'My brother has acted nobly,' he began—'so generously that I can hardly speak of his conduct without making a fool of myself. He has made his will, Molly, and he has made me his heir.   I am a hard-hearted beast for feeling glad and proud at the idea of succeeding him.   He knows, poor dear fellow, that he has not long to live; and he has reconciled himself to the notion of my stepping into his shoes; and we have been over the map of the estate together, and he has talked to me a great deal of late about the property.'

'He has made his will,' said Molly; ' you are sure ?'

'I have his word for it, and he never told me a lie.'

' Well, you are a lucky man, Mark; ever so much luckier than you deserve to be.'

' I know that,' assented Mark meekly.

' Because a poor-spirited fellow like you would never do anything of his own account.   You would never be rich if somebody else's fortune did not drop into your lap.'

' Perhaps not, Molly; but you needn't taunt me with that.   I've run the risk of losing everything for your sake, and if it isn't in your nature to be grateful, you might at least strain a point and be civil.'

'Don't be cross, Mark,' she said, laying her hand upon his shoulder. 'Everything will be made up to us when we have got the estate. Won't the Camelot folks stare when I ride through the town in my carriage and pair! I would have six horses, just as old Sir Massey Lopes used to have, only it would be too much like a circus.'

'Six fiddlesticks!' muttered Mark. 'When I have a pack of hounds I'll drive you to the meet in my drag, if you like—for I mean to keep a drag and a good team; but, in an ordinary way, I should think a pony-chaise ought to satisfy you. But now, Molly, I am going to talk seriously. In the face of what I have just told you, with the certainty that you and I will be master and mistress here before we are many years older, I can't, and I won't, stand this masquerading of yours any longer. You and your widow's weeds must clear out of this immediately.'

'I understand,' **said** Molly, with a vixenish tightening of her lips. 'Now Miss Flossie is here *I* am in the way. I must make myself scarce immediately, in order to leave the coast clear for your flirtations.'

'Miss Flossie has nothing to do with it; and I've had too great a sickener of your sex to care about flirtations with a female angel,' retorted Mark, waxing savage. 'You must get out of this house at once, simply because it isn't decent that my wife should be here in such a position.'

'Well, Mark, only be reasonable,' pleaded Molly, with a sudden change from the virago to the turtle dove. 'I came here to watch your interests, and I am quite willing to go now that your interests are secured; but I can't go at an hour's notice. I must hatch some story to tell your sister. I must leave as respectably as I came. I'll say that I've received a letter from my aged mother in Lincolnshire, who is very ill, and wants me at home to nurse her. And I'll give your sister a month's notice.'

'A month!' ejaculated Mark. 'Why a month? Your aged mother would be dead and buried in that time!'

'Not if it was a chronic disorder—some lingering wasting complaint. A month is not long notice to give your sister, Mark, after she has made me a confidential servant. She would get suspicious and begin to make inquiries, perhaps, if I wanted to go away suddenly.'

'Well, I never could understand your motive for coming here, and I can no more fathom your motive for staying here. But all I have to say is, get out of the place as soon as you can.'

'Yes,' answered Molly, deep in thought, 'as soon as I can.'

She started at the ringing of a bell, and left him alone in the thickening darkness.

'I can't understand her,' he said to himself. 'I wish she was fair and above-board—like Flossie.'

And then he sighed, as he had sighed once before, at the mention of Flossie's name. It was not that he had any evil thought about her—any unholy dream or hope. It was only because she was so different from the woman to whom he had bound himself.

From that time forward Mark's mind was curiously divided between an honest affection for his brother and a natural pride in the things which were soon to be his own. He tried very hard to shut out of his mind that haunting idea of future

possession; but the stoicism required for such
self-abnegation was beyond the reach of Mark's
weak nature. In the stables, in the house, in the
grounds, he thought of the day when his own reign
should begin, and the level monotony which had
prevailed for the last half century should give
place to the animated life of a sporting squire's
household. He could not even keep silent as to
those schemes of alteration and improvement which
were for ever developing themselves in his brain.
He talked to the old head-groom of what he would
do in the stables if he were master: how he would
knock down this and clear away that, build loose
boxes instead of the old stalls, lift off dilapidated
roofs, give light and air to stables which, though
spacious enough to accommodate a stud of thirty
hunters, were little better than cattle-sheds for
arrangement and comfort; build kennels and cook-
ing-house in the paddock at the back of the stable-
yard, and make Place altogether worthy to be called
a gentleman's abode.

The old servants liked well enough to hear
him talk, and encouraged him to expatiate upon

his day-dream. **There was no** treason against
Vyvyan in such discourse. Every man must die
when his time comes; and, **as** there seemed no
likelihood of the elder brother becoming the father
of a family, Mark was accepted generally as the
future master of all things. **He** would be a pleasant easy-going ruler, people thought, and would
spend **his money in a** large open-handed manner,
which would allow of a good deal of its dropping
through his fingers into the pockets of other people.

While he is still flushed with **the** novelty of
his position as Vyvyan's declared heir, while his
spirits, despite his efforts to feel **sorry for** his
brother's shortened life, were **at** their highest, the
cup of hope was suddenly dashed from **his hand,**
and he felt that on him too fell the chill shade
of the common doom—that **he** too **was but** a passing shadow upon **life's changeful scene.**

He went into Vyvyan's den one morning, to
wait for his brother,. who had something to say
to him about one of the farms, and, being tired
and flushed with **an** early gallop upon the brown
cob, flung himself into Vyvyan's armchair, and took

a long pull of the honest brown October out of
Vyvyan's stout old George II. tankard. Refreshed
by the draught, he lay back in his chair indulging
in that day-dream which had beguiled him so often
of late—the thought of what he should do when
he was master. Thus, with his eyes half closed,
he rested his tired limbs, and dreamed his dream
of horse and hound, spaniel and gun, otter-hunt
and steeplechase, without count of time, knowing
that Vyvyan would come to him as soon as he
had finished his interview with an offending tenant
who had been caught in the act of bartering the
straw which, in the form of manure, should have
enriched the land he rented. Vyvyan would come
in due time; and in the mean while the day-dream
went on, and Mark saw himself flying over a big
water-jump at Lanivet steeplechase, to the admira-
tion of the assembled multitude.

But, lo, what is this dull lethargy, never felt in
his life before, which steals over him in the midst of
his fancied triumph, and blots the visionary racecourse
and the visionary crowd from the scene, and clouds
the real parlour and the low red fire, till the smoulder-

ing logs look like patches of dull light seen afar off athwart a land of shadows? What is the meaning of this deathlike nausea, these cold drops of sweat that break out suddenly upon his brow, this dreadful sensation of sinking through the ground, there where he sits in his brother's armchair? Yes, as if the floor were empty space, and he was sinking slowly through into a pit beneath. What does it mean? Alas for those new-fledged hopes of his, he knows too well. That slowly-throbbing heart, with dull laborious beat, not twenty-five to the minute, gives him the answer to his question. The doom is on him too—not on his brother alone, but on him, the younger, as well as the elder. Hereditary heart-disease! As his father died in the prime and vigour of manhood, as he has been told his brother must die, so too must he die. This is his first warning. Fool, to have known of the doom of father and brother, and not to have expected the same fate for himself!

He sank into a sleep that was more like lethargy than slumber; and so Vyvyan found him half an hour afterwards.

'Why, Mark, old fellow, asleep at midday!' cried the Squire. 'This is taking life easily with a vengeance.'

And then, seeing the livid hue of the sleeper's face, Vyvyan took alarm. He bent over his brother, felt the cold forehead and hands, and shook him gently to rouse him.

'Wake up,' he said, taking a bottle from a cupboard by the fireplace, and pouring out half a tumbler of brandy. 'You must have a dose of my medicine.'

He had some difficulty in making his brother drink the brandy. His sleep was almost stupor. When he opened his eyes at last he looked at Vyvyan wonderingly, as at a stranger.

'Forty feet,' he said; 'not many horses would have cleared it as clean as that, would they, old flick?'

'Finish that brandy, Mark; you've been dreaming,' said Vyvyan.

'Yes; I dreamt I was going down to the bottomless pit.'

'What do you mean?'

'I was sinking through the floor, collapsing into my boots, melting into nothing. It was a disgusting sensation.'

'**Great God**!' cried Vyvyan. 'That is what I **feel** when I have my heart-attacks.'

'And this was heart. We're both in the same boat, Vyvyan,' said **Mark** gloomily. 'You needn't have troubled to make a **will in** my favour. We're both entered **for the same** race, old fellow; and who can tell which horse will be first to pass the judge's chair?'

'This is horrible,' sighed Vyvyan, throwing himself upon the sofa. 'I never contemplated the possibility of such a thing. The thought of my **poor** father's untimely death never suggested a fear for my own life, or for yours. I know that consumption is hereditary. Wherever there is *that* taint in the blood, there is cause for fear. But heart-disease— **can** that too be a heritage from father to son? **And in my** father's **case** there was no warning. **I never** heard him complain. Have you never felt this before, Mark?'

'Never, so help me, Heaven!'

'What had you been doing this morning? Over-exerting yourself, I daresay. It was a long day on that black horse you bought me that brought on my first attack.'

'Yes, I suppose that was what did it for me. I had a tremendous gallop over the moor this morning. I wanted to take it out of Fiddlehead before I rode him with Flossie. He's one of the best horses I ever rode, but a confounded puller. I felt dead-beat when I came in here, and as dry as a limekiln. I nearly emptied your tankard.'

'Well, you see, Mark,' said the Squire thought-fully, 'we are both mortal. While we are building our barns and adding to our lands, the fiat goes forth, "Thou fool"—you know the rest. We must look the future in the face, Mark. If I had a son—or you had a son—I would bow to Fate, and make no moan. But to think that the estate should go to a beggarly heir-at-law—Jack Philip, of Liskeard—who will take out a patent, and call himself Philip Penruth, perhaps, and think himself as big as the biggest of us! The thought of that fellow is enough to make me alter my will, and leave the land to my wife, even though I know she would hand over everything to her Indian free-lance, after wearing widow's weeds for a year or so.'

'Don't do that,' gasped Mark, still faint from the prostration of his attack. 'Who knows how long you and I may live? You may have a son—or I. Don't alter your will; let that stand. Anything—even a scurvy fellow like Jack Philip—would be better than that your widow's second husband should be master here. He would be the worst of aliens.'

'Not worse than a beggarly attorney in a beggarly country town,' answered Vyvyan testily. 'I would rather the Crown had my estate than Jack Philip. Well, I can leave it all to a charity, that's one comfort.'

'Let your will stand, Vyvyan. Be reasonable. I may have a secret to tell you before long—a secret that may alter the state of affairs.'

'I understand,' said Vyvyan; 'you are thinking of getting married. Well, go on and prosper. You are eleven years my junior. Take this business of to-day as a warning to live quietly, and perhaps you may spin out the thread of life to a decent length. We mustn't let fears or fancies kill us.'

'Mine was no fancy,' said Mark despondently; 'it was the most horrible sensation I ever had in my life.'

'Didcott has advised me to leave off beer, and drink nothing but weak brand-and-water,' said Vyvyan, ringing the bell for a fresh supply of home-brewed; 'but I am a creature of habit, and must live my life my own way, even at the risk of shortening it. I couldn't get on without my morning tankard.'

Vyvyan thought much of his brother's illness. The idea that his race was destined to perish out of the land haunted him like a nightmare. It had been hard for him to reconcile himself to the thought that he himself must go, that another must be master of the things he loved, though that other one were his own brother; but that they should go to an alien was a far bitterer thought.

'If Mark would but marry!'

What, to rear a sickly race—children tainted with hereditary disease? How could he tell upon what future generations this doom might descend? **If** upon him and upon his brother, why not upon his brother's children?

'We are an expiring race,' he said to himself; '**the** canker is at the root, and the tree must **fall.**'

His conduct to his brother after this time showed more affection, in his own rough and rugged way, than it had ever done before. As he had pitied himself, when the knowledge of his doom was first revealed to him, so now he pitied his brother.

'Still in the prime of life, and taking life **so** lightly,' he thought. 'It must be harder for him than for me to know that his days are to be short in the land.'

A change came over Mark after that sudden shock, which reminded him of life's uncertainty. He **said** nothing to the woman who had hitherto shared most of his secrets. He shrank, just as Vyvyan **had** done, from talking of this thing; but he thought of it day and night.

The images of those three little lads at St. Columb haunted him at this time, and were his chief

LIBRARY
UNIVERSITY OF ILLINOIS

source of trouble. Something must be done for them. If he were to die before his elder brother, and Vyvyan were to do what he had threatened— leave his estate to a charity? Where then would be home and shelter and means for those three curly pates, who had composed themselves into such pretty pictures, climbing about their father's knees in the winter fireglow? Those chubby cheeks and innocent laughing eyes were always before Mark's mental vision in these days. Something must be done— nay, one thing alone could be done. His brother must be told of the existence of the boys, and of their claim upon his bounty, their right to call themselves by his name.

'He will be furiously angry—he will turn me out of his house, perhaps,' thought Mark; 'but I sha'n't mind that, if he will only be good to them. I am the sinner.'

And then Mark remembered with a heavy heart how one awful passage in Holy Writ declared that the sins of the fathers should be visited upon the children. And he had of his own experience seen how the thing does happen in life, and how the innocent offspring have to pay the penalty of the parents' crime.

'But mine is not a crime,' argued Mark. 'At the worst it is but an error. Why should I be afraid to tell him?'

Why, indeed, save for the reason that some natures are fashioned so limply that they recoil from every act which requires a bracing up of nerves and will, and a bold face-to-face encounter with stern necessity. Mark knew that if he confessed his fault to his brother there would be a storm of anger to be lived through, and Mark loved fair weather. Yet he had now come to a crisis in which he told himself that Vyvyan must learn the truth. The only question was as to when and how the revelation was to be made.

'If I were to tell Molly that I'm likely to die suddenly, as my father did, she wouldn't let me have an hour's peace,' he thought. 'She would worry me into my grave.'

For this reason, therefore, if for this only, he told Molly nothing of his illness that morning in Vyvyan's den.

Time was hurrying on, the leaves were falling, the days shortening, the mists of November creeping over the hill, and the date of Mrs. Morris's departure was fast approaching; much to the annoyance of Miss Penruth, who declared that she should never again get a maid to suit her so well.

'She is a most admirable person,' she said, in the family circle. 'I only wish that people of superior station were her intellectual equals or had her sound ideas of right and wrong. All I wonder is how such a person as Mrs. Nichols could have become acquainted with a woman of such a type.'

Mark heard, and shivered with apprehension. If ever the truth about Mrs. Morris should come to be known, how would Miss Penruth be induced to pardon an imposture which must needs make her appear ridiculous!

Meanwhile life went on smoothly enough in the dull old house. Mrs. Trevornock was happy with her elder daughter; she sat by the drawing-room fire working, or went for a drive in the landau, or wrote an occasional letter to aunt Sophia, expatiating upon the splendour of her daughter's surroundings and the sterling goodness of her son-in-law. Vyvyan spent a good deal of his time alone in his study, making business a pretext for seclusion. Flossie contrived to be out as much as possible, and indoors amused herself tolerably with reading novels, petting Mark's dogs, and teasing Mark, whom she appeared to consider sent into this world for her to worry. Yet if to be so worried had been the darkest feature in Mark's life, he would hardly have deemed existence a burden.

It was within three days of Mrs. Morris's departure, and the rest of the household, with a natural detestation of new favourites, were all rejoicing in their impending loss. People who keep themselves apart from the common herd may be respected, but they are rarely liked; and Mrs. Morris had lived in a retirement which was taken as a tacit assertion of her superiority to her fellow-workers.

'She must take her meals in her own room, forsooth,' said Gilmore the housekeeper, mother to Mrs. Penruth's own maid; 'as if we weren't good enough for her company; and she looks down upon chapel-people, if you please. Well, she be going, and joy go with her! I'd rather have Thomasine Tudway's faults than her virtues, though Miss Penruth do set such store by her.'

Vyvyan sat alone by his study fire after breakfast upon this November morning. It was some time since he had had any return of the old attack, yet he was far from well. He had never recovered the strength he lost while he lay prostrate with rheumatic pain and low fever. The change from a life spent for the most part in open-air exercise, with ample occupation for mind and body, to dull brooding days by a fireside, overshadowed and possessed by one fixed idea, is a change that no man can undergo without mental and physical deterioration. Vyvyan Penruth was no more like the man he had been four months ago than he was like Hercules; and it was when nerves and body were in this degenerate state that the heaviest blow which was ever aimed at him fell with crushing weight upon his dejected soul.

The morning mail brought him only one letter—a letter addressed in an unknown hand, the charac-

terless copper-plate style of **a tradesman's circular,**
the post-mark, Camelot.

'An account of some kind,' he thought, and list-
lessly tore open the envelope.

This was the letter :

'Take a plain warning from one who **is** a friend
to you and your family. Your wife's lover **is at Rock-**
port, and it may not be very long before he and she
are over the border. They have been seen together.
Ask your father-in-law's late clerk, Lewis Maul-
ford, how these two young people were together at
Southampton before the Captain sailed for India—
how they were seen in the town—and how the **lady**
went back to London in a third-class carriage, **veiled**
and muffled, to escape notice. Curious, **to say the**
least of it; but Mrs. **T.** brought up her girls curi-
ously. This is meant **in all** friendliness. It may
not be too late to save **the lady's** reputation and your
honour. Forewarned **is** forearmed.'

'An **anonymous** letter! a tissue of lies, most
likely,' **Vyvyan told** himself; ' or of truths **so dis-**
torted **as to be** more false than unalloyed false-
hood.'

Yet while he argued with himself he believed, and his heart hardened itself against the wife who had given him duty and obedience, but not love.

That Major Leland was at Rockport, he knew. Priscilla had taken care to keep him informed on that point. But that Barbara and he had met? No, he could hardly believe that. She had never been out alone within his knowledge; but she and Flossie had gone for long drives across the moor, in the pony-carriage, unattended. A girl of Flossie's stamp would connive at any wrongdoing, out of mere frivolity. Yes, they had met, no doubt, those three, and Flossie's presence was but a poor safe-guard.

And the story of a meeting at Southampton years ago. That was a darker history, perhaps. That involved character—was in itself enough to blight a woman's reputation.

'If there is any truth in that charge, what can I think of her, how can I believe in her henceforward?' he asked himself.

And then, pale with suppressed passion, with dry throat and parched lips, he stretched out his hand mechanically to the old silver tankard that held his morning draught—always put ready for him on his table at eleven o'clock—and drank with feverish avidity nearly to the bottom of the cup.

CHAPTER IV.

VYVYAN PENRUTH paced up and down his room with the anonymous letter crushed in his bony hand.

How much did it mean, or how little? Unversed though he was in the ways of the world outside his own small kingdom, he was not so weak as to surrender his opinions—his own honest faith in his wife's goodness and truth—at the first attack of a nameless assailant. Yet, granted that this anonymous slanderer was a scoundrel, here was a plain fact stated, open to proof, which if true would stamp his wife as unworthy of the confidence he had given her.

Alone at Southampton with her lover; for how long or how short a time? She had been seen with him at Southampton before he sailed. That was all the letter stated. But the secret return—muffled and veiled—implied that their meeting had been stealthy, in some wise shameful.

His wife—the woman whose girlish innocence,
whose childlike simplicity of mind, he had rever-
enced, in his own rough way—his wife alone with
her lover in a strange town, the observed of un-
friendly eyes, stealing back to London like a guilty
creature.

'I cannot believe it,' he said to himself; 'I will
show her the letter. I will hear what she has to say
to the charge. Her own lips shall justify or con-
demn her.'

And then he remembered Barbara's curious
antipathy to Maulford—a dislike which seemed so
irrational, so unmerited by its object.

'Ask Maulford how they were together at Southampton,' said the letter. Maulford was indicated as
the possessor of facts that condemned her.

Was it for this she disliked him?

'I will ask her what it all means,' Vyvyan said
to himself again, staggered somewhat by this idea
about Maulford. 'I will wring the truth from her
somehow.'

Suddenly the letter dropped from his relaxing
fingers, and he flung himself heavily on the sofa.

It was the old feeling—the death-like torpor, the icy-
sweat, the dimness of vision, the hideous sensation
of sinking through the couch on which he lay ; and
this time the symptoms had a triple power, and he
felt this must be death.

What did it mean ?   In this room—always in
this room—at the same hour—at the same, or
nearly the same, interval after his morning drink of
beer.

Could disease be so mathematically periodic in
its recurrence ? observe the same hour ? seize him
always in the same spot ?

'What if it were not disease, but poison ?' he
thought, with a dull horror creeping through his
veins.

He was not wanted in the world.   Indeed, knowing, as he knew, that George Leland was home from
India—close at his door—he could hardly doubt that
he was very much wanted out of the world.   His
wife had been sweet and gentle and tender in all
her dealings with him.   What of that ?   Women as
soft-handed and as tender have been false as hell.

Didcott had told him that these symptoms meant

heart-disease ; but this proved **nothing.** Your doctor **rarely finds out** that his patient has been poisoned till after his death. He stands by and watches
the case, and wonders a little, and **has** a general
feeling that things are not going on pleasantly ; and
then by and by there is a post-mortem, **and a** scien-
tific analyst finds traces of poison ; **and the** family
doctor says he had thought so, and the consulting
physician deposes that there were grounds for **grave**
suspicion, **but** that those grounds were not quite
strong enough **for a** cautious medical man, with **an**
eye to his practice, **to proceed upon.**

Poisoned ! He remembered how Mark had **been**
seized in exactly the same way, with precisely the
same symptoms, in that room, after emptying yonder tankard—the honest old tankard, dinted with
service like a soldier's breastplate, **which** his father
and grandfather had drunk out of before him ; the
tankard **which, in** more convivial times, had passed
from hand to hand, as a loving-cup, after boisterous
hunting dinners.

Poisoned ! **Yes, his strength had been slowly**
sapped, his nerves had been shattered **by a** myste-

rious malady. His heart had beaten with the steady
jog-trot pace of old in the intervals of the disease;
but when the fit seized him, in a moment the pulse
grew slow and feeble, and the dull languor that was
like death slackened the beating of the heart.

He was to be got rid of—not too suddenly, lest
his death, being so convenient and happy an event
for his widow, should give rise to suspicion. Some
poison must be found which would simulate a mortal
malady, and then, when the belief in that malady
was established, the dose was to be made stronger,
and the victim was to die.

Major Leland was near at hand, waiting for the
end, ready to profit by it, in all likelihood the insti-
gator of the crime.

He thought in gasps—disjointedly—his brain
clouded by that dreadful lethargic heaviness which
bound him to his sofa. Then, with a great effort,
he raised himself on his elbow, and stretched out his
hand to the bell. He was just able to reach it.

'She shall know that I have found her out,' he
muttered; 'I will not die like a poisoned rat in a
hole—die, and make no sign.'

' Send your mistress to me,' he said to the butler, who appeared at the door.

' Yes, sir.   I beg your pardon, sir, are you ill ?'

' No.   Send your mistress directly.'

Dickson retired, scared by his master's ashy face and feeble tones.   He found Barbara with Mrs. Trevornock in the morning-room, and delivered his message.   Mrs. Penruth hurried to the study.

' Vyvyan,' she cried, seeing her husband lying on the sofa, prostrate, helpless, as he had lain that other day, ' how white and faint you look !   Let me give you some brandy.'

' No, there would be death in it, perhaps.   I want to ask you a question.   Stand there, where I can see your face ; there, facing the light.   Great God, what purity and candour beam in your eyes !   I have had a letter about you.'

' A letter !   From whom ?'

' From somebody who knew you before you were married.   Tell me now, Mrs. Penruth, how far had matters gone with you and your lover before he went to India ?   I ought to have asked that question before I married you, ought I not ?   But you see I

was a fool from the beginning; I trusted you blindly.
You were with your lover at Southampton before he
sailed ?'

'I went to see him on the day he sailed, to say
good-bye to him.'

'O, you went only on the day he sailed. You
were not staying at Southampton with him ?'

'Vyvyan !' see cried, with an indignant look.

'You ought not to be surprised at the question.
A lady who goes alone to a strange town to see her
lover, and is seen with him there, must expect to be
suspected.'

'I see,' said Barbara, 'Mr. Maulford has told you.
He saw me part from Captain Leland when the
Hesper sailed; he put me into the train. Was it
wrong to go and say good-bye to him on that last
day, Vyvyan? If it was, I did not know it. He
was my future husband, as I believed then, and we
were to be parted for years. My mother and sister
know how and when I went, how long I was away.
You can question them, if you like.'

'You are a lovely piece of innocence,' gasped
Vyvyan, succumbing again to that deadly faintness;

'and you have planned things cleverly for your lover and yourself. But perhaps even this last dose of poison was not quite strong enough, and I may survive it. Give me the brandy bottle—if—if that is not poisoned too.'

'Vyvyan, dear Vyvyan, your mind is wandering,' she said, filling a glass of brandy, and holding it to his lips with a shaking hand.

'Ah, your hand trembles ; you are not altogether stone. You can poison a husband in cold blood, see him die by inches before your face, make believe to pity him ; yet, when the end comes, you tremble.'

Frightened out of her senses, Barbara rang the bell with a desperate peal.

'Send for Mr. Didcott as fast as the groom can ride !' she said to the alarmed Dickson. 'Tell my mother—no, my sister—to come here directly. Not a word to Mrs. Trevornock.'

She knelt by her husband's side, and wiped the icy drops from his brow. Passion had given him a force that triumphed over his physical weakness ; but this spurious strength was now exhausted, and he lay in a state of lethargy, heedless of what was pass-

ing round him. Barbara could only force a few drops
of brandy between his livid lips. The pupils of his
eyes were dilated, and the whole countenance had an
awful look, which to Barbara, who had never seen
death, seemed like death itself.

Flossie came running in breathless.

'What's the matter?' she asked.

'Vyvyan is ill—dreadfully ill. O Flossie, he has
talked to me about my journey to Southampton as if
it were a wicked act, as if I were a lost creature for
going there. You—you can tell him that I only left
you in the early morning, just to see George once
more; that I was home with you again in the evening; that I had no thought of wrong-doing; no idea
that any one could think evil of me for going.'

'Of course not,' cried Flossie sharply. 'Brother-
in-law, you ought to be ashamed of yourself for
going on in such a horrid way. But, good gracious,
how ill he looks! too ill to understand me, poor
creature! What does it mean?'

'I have seen him like this before, but the attack
was not so bad. His mind has been wandering—he
told me he was being poisoned; said that I was

poisoning him. O Flossie, Flossie, what shall I do?'
cried Barbara, bursting into tears.

'Do? Why, send for a doctor. If we were in a
civilised place, I should say send for a policeman.'

'I have sent for the doctor. Miss Penruth ought
to be told Go and fetch her, Flossie. God help
me, I haven't a friend in the world!'

'Fetch Miss Penruth, indeed!' muttered Flossie,
as she tore up to her own room. 'Miss Penruth
would have to be a great deal further off before
I'd do it. No, I'll fetch a man—a man with a heart
and brains—who can tell that poor girl what she
ought to do, and protect her against a madman; for
it looks as if my brother-in-law had gone clean out of
his wits.'

Flossie always dressed quickly for her excur-
sions on horseback; but to-day she put herself into
her riding-gear with an amazing rapidity. The
habit fitted well and easily, though it was made by a
Camberwell tailor; the cavalier hat was perched
jauntily on the pretty head; and Flossie ran down-
stairs looking as neat and trim as if she had dressed
in the most leisurely way. She had sent Gilmore

to the stable to order Pepper to be ready in an instant, an order that could only be executed in a
modified manner; but the stablemen had done their
best, for when she went into the yard she found one
of them puffing and grumbling as he tugged at
Pepper's girths, protesting that 'this yere 'oss do
blow hisself out as if he had a blacksmith's bellers
inside him.'

'You hain't goin' after doctor, be ye, miss?' said
the man who mounted Flossie; 'becos Sanderson
galloped off to Camelot on the black mare twenty
minutes ago, and he'll be half-way there by this
time.'

'No, Peter, I'm only going for a ride,' Flossie
answered innocently.

She jogged on at a sober pace so long as she
was within sight of the stablemen, who had grouped
themselves at the gate to watch her, with that re-
markable interest in passing events which is only
another name for idleness; but when the curve of
the road took her out of their view she gave the
reins a shake, and Pepper a slash which sent him
flying.

And when she was once on the moor, with the crisp hillocky turf under her horse's hoofs, did not this young lady go! Over hillock and hollow, heather and granite, went Pepper, like a horse with charmed legs, knuckling over and pulling himself up now and again with marvellous cleverněss, and so on to a smooth stretch of turf beside the road, where Pepper went as evenly as a racer. Then a pause to breathe the horse, a little hand playing pit-a-pat on his neck, an encouraging assurance that he was 'a good horse, a dear old Pepper;' and anon, while beguiled by these blandishments he was lapsing into a comfortable crawl, another rousing slash of the whalebone, and away again, up hill and down hill, over gorse and quagmire at a flying canter. And thus and thus, till they come to the edge of the moor above Rockport, and see the little harbour lying in the cleft of the cliffs below them, while Pepper scents the salt sea-breeze, and tosses his mane and paws the ground as if he were eager to be off again.

Flossie trots him briskly down the hill, which would be dangerously steep if the road did not wind

corkscrew fashion down to the deep hollow where the
little harbour nestles like a tiny world at the bottom
of a pit, a mere dimple on the earth's surface, yet
with its births and deaths, its wooing and marrying,
its friendlinesses and its feuds, as complete in itself
as if it were as big as the universe.

Here, face to face with a watermill, stands the
homely comfortable Waterloo Inn, sheltered by steep
green hills from every wind that blows; a blessed
haven from the storms of life. How sweet a resting-
place to the soldier, after forced marches under torrid
skies, brief slumbers by the wayside, made restless
by the howl of the jackal, the possibility of the cobra,
watching and fasting and toil and danger!

All these were past, and George Leland lounged
in the porch of the Waterloo Inn, smoking his che-
root and looking idly across the narrow harbour to
the heathery ridge above, where the dark moor
sloped off to unknown distances. He was roused
from a gloomy reverie—the despondent survey of a
world emptied of all delight—by the sharp click-
clack of a horse's hoofs on the hard road, and on
turning his eyes that way he perceived Flossie's

blue riding-habit and the **bulky form of the** useful Pepper. He **threw** away his cigar, and hastened **to** meet the solitary Amazon.

'**Were** you coming to see me?' he exclaimed. '**How** good of you! But how agitated **you look!** Is there anything wrong?'

'Tremendously wrong!' panted Flossie. 'That unfortunate brother-in-law of mine seems to have gone·out of his mind. He was in a kind of fit when I came away, and he had been raving dreadfully—**saying that he** was poisoned, accusing Barbara. I want you to **come with** me. We are three helpless women, ma, Bab, and I, in that lonely house, with**out a** friend; for I consider Miss Penruth an **enemy,** and I can't count Mark, for he's out all day, and of course, however good-natured he may **be,** he would go over to his brother's side **in a family quarrel.** So I want you to come: you will be some one on our side—a soldier, brave, determined, ready to fight for us. O Major Leland, *is* my sister to be accused of poisoning people?' gasped Flossie, in a tumult **of** indignation.

'By no one but a lunatic,' answered Leland

wrathfully. 'I'll come as soon as I can get a horse saddled.'

There were post-horses at the Waterloo, and a couple of good hacks into the bargain, one of which carried the landlord, who was a welter-weight. This powerful brute George Leland helped to saddle, and he was mounted and ready to start in less than ten minutes. Then walking their horses up the hill, the better to cover the ground when they got to the top, the Major asked Flossie for further information as to the state of affairs at Place.

'Has Mr. Penruth ever treated your sister unkindly before to-day?' he asked.

'Never. He has been the best of husbands—a little grumpy, you know; but that's his way, and it is a grumpiness that does nobody harm.. He is not a bit like that horrid sister of his, whose chief desire is to domineer over everybody, and to regulate us all as if she were Charles V., and we were so many clocks. Vyvyan has been kind to us all—I mean ma, Bab, and me. He gave me ten pounds to buy this very habit, when I was going back to Camberwell after our first visit, and when I had been wearing a hideous old-fashioned thing of Miss Penruth's which was so tight in the **arm-holes as** to be absolute **torture**, to say nothing of the sense of obligation, which **was worse.** No,' resumed Flossie, after this excursus; ' I don't believe he ever spoke unkindly to Barbara before this day, and I **feel sure he** must have gone clean out of his wits.'

' Did your sister tell you to come for me?' asked the Major, faltering a little.

' Not she! **Bab** never had a business-like idea in her life. Bab is the sort of person who in a great calamity would sit upon the ground, and cry, " Allah is good! Kismet!" or some nonsense of that kind. Was it not I **who** always had to tackle Mr. T. ? and even now, in spite of the income Barbara allows **us,** I would get the Queen's taxes and poor-rates out of him if ma would let me. Barbara has not an idea that I have come for you. She told me to go and fetch Miss Penruth. I should like to have seen myself doing it! " I'd see her further first, and then I wouldn't,"' added Flossie, quoting the burlesque of *Conrad and Medora*, **which** was just now the rage in London.

They were at the top of the hill by this time.

'Now, Flossie,' said the Major, 'if you're sure of your seat and are not afraid of a hand-gallop, show me the way to Place.'

'All right,' answered the girl, bracing her bridle, and giving Pepper a smart lash on his shoulder. Away they went, as if they were riding a steeple-chase, skimming cleverly over hillocky ground, plunging up to the horses' hocks through bog and slush; then spinning away swifter than ostriches across the good firm turf, here and there leaping a low furze-bush in the excitement of the chase; and so to the open gates of the oak plantation, and on at a sharp trot to the house.

Here all was confusion. Vyvyan still lay in that awful death-like lethargy into which he had fallen when his passion had exhausted itself. He had been carried to his own room and laid upon his own bed, and the household had done what they could for him, but without avail. Mrs. Morris, as a person accustomed to sickness, had been called upon, Miss Penruth standing by and giving orders, but doing nothing. The messenger had returned from Camelot with the news that Mr. Didcott was from home, and likely to be away all day, as he had a difficult case at a farmhouse nine miles from the town, St. Columb way. The man had been despatched to Launceston straightway on a fresh horse, to get a doctor from that town, but there was no chance of his being back for the next hour.

In the absence of medical advice Mrs. Morris had taken upon herself to protest against brandy being given to the patient, although Barbara declared that it had cured him upon a previous occasion.

'Nothing worse than brandy where the head is affected,' said Mrs. Morris decidedly. 'Inflammatory.'

Miss Penruth, who had a natural bent to teetotalism, and looked upon all use of alcohol as intemperance, supported her confidential servant in this view of the case ; so no brandy was administered to Vyvyan after those few drops which Barbara had forced between his lips. He lay like a log, the scared wife and sister watching him, the old butler in attendance, with the vague idea of doing something useful presently, and of all the group only Mrs. Morris self-possessed or capable. She sat

by the bed as calmly as if she had been watching
by a child's cradle while it slept the happy sleep
of healthful infancy.

Barbara paced up and down the room—now wish-
ing that the doctor were come, now wondering why
Mark was not there—praying inwardly for help.

Upon this scene entered George Leland and
Flossie, who had heard from the footman below the
state of things up-stairs.

'I hope you won't be angry with me,' said Flossie.
'I rode over to Rockport to fetch Major Leland; for
I thought he would be able to advise you.'

Barbara turned to her lover with a look—first
surprise mingled with fear, then ineffable confidence.
He had come as her friend, her protector, her guide,
her counsellor.

'O,' she cried piteously, 'help us if you can; my
poor husband is dying, and no one knows what to do
to save him. We have no doctor, and no one to
advise.'

It was afternoon, and the westward-sloping sun
was shining full into the room. George Leland
looked round at all the faces, taking in every detail

of the scene, every variety of expression in the actors, with a swift scrutiny.   He was a man accustomed to emergencies, skilled in reading character, a man who had led a hard life and seen strange things and strange people.   He had been judge and jury, prosecutor and advocate, in the days of his Indian commissionership.   He had dealt largely with cheats and rascals, and he knew the seamy side of human nature as well as any one.

He read the story of those faces.   Miss Penruth fretful, sanctimonious, inclined to be malignant. The old butler a model of faithful imbecility.   These were as easy to read as the big letters in a baby's alphabet.   But here was a countenance whose meaning was printed in a different type, and needed a longer scrutiny ; this calm hard face framed in a widow's cap, these bugle-bright black eyes which shifted nervously as they looked at him, these thin cruel lips closed as tight as metal springs, yet agitated by a nervous quivering for a moment or two while he watched the face.

'Tell me what is the matter, Mrs. Penruth,' he said gently, going up to the bedside, where his rival lay motionless, seemingly senseless. 'Tell me all you can. I am half a doctor; for it was my luck to see a good deal of sickness at the infirmary where I had temporary quarters while I was superintending the building of a new hospital, to say nothing of my experience on long marches, when I have had to be surgeon as well as captain.'

Barbara, trembling a little, told him as much as she knew of the symptoms of the case; told him how she had seen her husband affected months ago in a similar manner, but less violently; how a glass of brandy had then revived him.

'Indeed! And you have been giving him brandy now, I suppose?'

'No,' said Barbara; 'Mrs. Morris thought it wiser not.'

'Give me the bottle, please,' said the Major, with an observant look at the widow, who was a shade paler than when he entered the room. 'Your experience should have prevailed over Mrs. Morris's wisdom, Mrs. Penruth.'

With the help of Dickson, who was adipose and jelly-fish-like in build, but who had a heart of gold,

Major Leland contrived to force half a tumbler of brandy down Vyvyan's throat. Then he looked at his eyes, saw the unnatural dilatation of the pupil, felt his pulse, heart, the temperature of his skin, noted the swollen lips.

'I have seen just such symptoms in a case of snake-bite,' he said. 'Have you any ammonia in the house?'

Miss Penruth's mind had been curiously divided between a sense of relief in the fact that some one had come to her brother's assistance and intense indignation at his impertinence in coming. She now opened her lips for the first time since Major Leland's entrance, and in somewise relaxed the stony stare with which she had been regarding him.

'I think I have a little,' she said, 'in my dressing-case. Go and fetch it, Morris,—a small stoppered bottle, labelled sal volatile.'

The inestimable Morris obeyed, moving slowly and rigidly, as if she had been a mechanical figure.

CHAPTER V.

'FLOSSIE tells me that Mr. Penruth talked about
being poisoned,' said George Leland, in a low voice
to Barbara, while Mrs. Morris was gone to fetch
the ammonia. 'Is that true?'

'Yes; he said he had been poisoned—he talked
wildly about poison.'

'I am hardly surprised, for the symptoms look
terribly like that, and nothing else.'

'Good Heavens!' cried Barbara; 'but who could
give him poison? How could poison come in his
way?'

'Accidentally, perhaps. One can never tell.
You cannot do wrong in giving him powerful stimulants. It looks like a case of narcotic poison. I
saw exactly these symptoms—the same look in the
eyes, the same lethargy—in a man who was being
treated for heart-disease in the infirmary I was
telling you about. The surgeon had given him

gentle doses of an infusion of digitalis—foxglove, you know—as a sedative; and one night the fellow had an attack of palpitation, and, believing that if a little of the stuff gave him a little relief, a good deal of it would cure him altogether, he got up while every one in the ward was asleep, and emptied the bottle. He was pretty near death, I can tell you; and it was only by dosing him with ammonia and strong coffee that the doctor brought him round.'

'And you think Vyvyan has been taking some preparation of foxglove?' said Barbara, standing by the bed, chafing her husband's icy hands, while Miss Penruth stood on the opposite side, listening intently.

Mrs. Morris came in at this moment, followed closely by Mark, who hurried into the room in an agitated manner, whip in hand, having jumped off his horse a minute ago, and rushed straight from the stable-yard.

'Is he better?' he cried.

'He is still living,' answered Priscilla. 'We must be thankful for that. This gentleman, an old friend of Mrs. Penruth's, is trying to render us assistance in the absence of any doctor.'

'Has no doctor come?'

'Not yet. Mr. Didcott was away.'

'Yes, William told me. You have sent to Launceston, I suppose?'

'Yes; the messenger ought to be back by this time. O, dear, dear!' exclaimed Priscilla, watching Major Leland, who, with Barbara's help, was administering a dose of ammonia, 'I trust in God we are doing what is right. O Major Leland, you are not tampering with that precious life? you are sure that this is proper treatment?'

'I am doing what I would do if Mr. Penruth were my own father,' answered Leland; 'I should act in exactly the same manner if his life were of all lives the most precious to me.'

'How long has he been like this?' asked Mark, looking down at his brother.

'Since twelve o'clock. It was a sudden seizure. Mrs. Penruth was with him.'

'It is his heart that is affected,' said Mark, looking at Major Leland. 'For mercy's sake don't try to doctor him unless you know all about heart-disease !'

'This is no heart-disease,' answered Leland. 'Your brother is suffering from the effect of some powerful narcotic poison.'

'Poison !' cried Mark.   'How should he be poisoned ?'

'It is for you and Mrs. Penruth to find out that.'

'But he has suffered from such attacks—not so bad as this ; but the same kind of thing—for the last three months.   The doctor examined him, and told him that his heart was out of order.   The complaint is hereditary.   My father dropped down dead.   I have had the same kind of attack.'

'Then I think you must have taken the same kind of poison.'

Mark stared at him with a ghastly face, remembering that draught of beer out of his brother's tankard, and how it was only on that one occasion he had been attacked by his brother's malady.

'Great God !' he cried, 'if this is true, there must be some devil in the house !'

He looked round among the assembled faces,
aghast with horror—looked in vacant wonder, till
one face amidst them all, standing vividly out from
the rest, as if the dark secrets of the soul behind
it were written upon it in characters of fire, riveted
his gaze.

Which of all those faces looked like a devil's?
This one, most surely; this rigid countenance lit
by the serpent's glittering eyes, with the cruel
downward curve of the serpent's venomous mouth;
this face which had once seemed so fair in Mark
Penruth's sight, a face to peril fortune for; this
face set off and garnished by the widow's cap, the
sleek banded hair; this bloodless countenance in
which the livid hue of the cheeks seemed more unnatural because of the one central spot of hectic
which burned on each, like the print of a Satanic
kiss.

Mark staggered to his brother's bedside, and
flung himself down against the pillows, interposing
his body between Vyvyan's motionless figure and
all the rest of the world. For some moments he
remained thus, speechless, leaning against his bro-

ther, as a dog might have done, with **something of a**
dog's fidelity; **and as** he hung over the sick man*
thus, old memories of boyish days came back to him;
the time when he had revered and admired Vyvyan
as the tall grown-up brother—a young man while
Mark was still a child; the day when Vyvyan had
mounted him on a rat of an Exmoor pony and taken
him for his **first** ride, with a leading-rein. **Many**
a brotherly kindness, many an act of love flashed
across Mark's memory as he leant upon his **brother's**
bed in the fast darkening room.

'If there has **been foul play,'** he muttered
hoarsely, '**I will not** spare the poisoner. No; **I**
will not spare !'

The powerful stimulants were beginning to take
effect. The patient stirred and moaned in his sleep.

They watched him thus **for a long and anxious**
hour, watched and waited in silence, while George
Leland administered brandy or ammonia from time
to time, and kept Mrs. Morris hard at work heating
flannels and filling hot-water bottles to be applied
to the patient's feet. **The** sluggish heart **began to**
move a little more naturally, the cold sweat cleared

off the pale fixed face, the swollen lips lost something of their livid hue, and a faint tinge of red came back to the hollow cheeks.

'I believe he will live through it,' said George Leland at last.

'Could not an emetic have been given him?' asked Mark.

'Yes, if any one had thought of it when the attack began ; but after three or four hours it would be fatal. I remember what the surgeon at· our infirmary said about it. I am simply copying his treatment. He saved his man, and, please God, we shall save ours.'

'You are a good fellow,' said Mark.

'I am Mrs. Penruth's faithful friend,' answered Leland ; 'that is my highest merit.'

After this there was silence for some time, Mark not stirring from his post at his brother's side, Barbara sitting close by, George Leland standing at the foot of the bed. On the other side sat Miss Penruth and Mrs. Morris, the former seeking consolation alternately from an open book of *Precious Balms for Broken Spirits*, by an unknown Colonial bishop, and a silver vinaigrette. Flossie was with her mother in Barbara's dressing-room, the door of communication being open, to allow of the younger lady peeping in every five minutes or so, and asking in a whisper of nobody in particular,

'Is he getting better?'

He was so much better presently that he turned on his pillow, opened his eyes, and recognised his brother.

'What, Mark, old fellow, is that you?'

'Yes, Vyvyan. Thank God, you know me.'

Vyvyan tried to raise himself; but the effort brought on intense giddiness.

'No,' he muttered; 'I must lie here like a log, lie here till I die.'

He took no notice of Major Leland, whose tall figure was partly hidden by the curtain. His dull eyes took heed of no one but his brother, whose arm he could feel round him.

Just at this moment the Launceston doctor entered—a middle-aged man, bald, spectacled, with a sagacious highly-polished brow, and a comfortable manner, soothing as a sedative.

To him Barbara turned with delight.

'Thank Heaven, you have come!' she said. 'This gentleman, Major Leland, has been helping us in our dreadful difficulty. He will tell you what he has done—what he thinks—'

'My dear lady, do not distress yourself,' said the doctor, looking round at the assembled multitude. 'The first thing will be to get the room cleared of everybody except yourself; and Major—er—Selim,' he added, making a dash at the name, 'who will kindly inform me what he has been doing.'

Mark turned from his brother's bed with a reluctant air, and walked slowly towards the door, looking curiously at Mrs. Morris as he passed her, like a man who has some fearful thought half-shaped in his brain.

Miss Penruth retired to the dressing-room where Flossie and her mother were waiting; but she did not go without a protest.

'Nobody can be more interested in my brother's health than I am,' she said; 'not even his wife; certainly not a stranger, however obliging.'

'My dear madam, I am aware how trying such an occasion must be for you, as well as for Mrs. Penruth; but quiet is indispensable. You may be within call. You shall have immediate information of any change in our patient.'

With these reassuring words the strange doctor, who seemed as much at home as if he had brought a generation or two of Penruths into the world, led Priscilla to the dressing-room, and dismissed her with a bland smile. Mrs. Morris had silently retired by the door leading into the gallery.

Then, having closed the door carefully, Mr. Fordyce, the Launceston doctor, came quietly back to the bedside, and proceeded to examine his patient.

Consciousness had in some degree returned. Vyvyan looked full at the stranger with glassy eyes, the pupils still unnaturally dilated.

'Mr. Penruth was seized with this disorder soon after noon to-day, I understand?' said Mr. Fordyce.

'Yes,' answered Barbara. 'He has had the same kind of illness before, but not with such violence. To-day he told me that he believed he was poisoned. When he said this I thought his mind

was affected; but Major Leland, who came over
from Rockport to help us in our distress, thinks
that my husband's illness is really caused by poison.'

'Pray, sir, may I ask what ground you have for
such an opinion?' Mr. Fordyce inquired coolly, as
he went on with his examination of the patient.

'Simply that I have seen a case of narcotic poisoning in which the symptoms were precisely similar.
I have applied the same remedies I saw used in that
case, and with the same happy effect. When I
came here two hours ago, Mr. Penruth was in a
deathlike stupor, his pulse hardly perceptible.'

'So you are Major Leland?' said Vyvyan, turning
his haggard face towards the soldier.

'What was the nature of the poison in the case
you speak of?' asked the doctor.

'Digitalis,' replied Leland; and then he went
on to describe the case at the Indian hospital.

Mr. Fordyce listened; but did not commit himself to an opinion, save to express mild approval of
Major Leland's treatment.

'You could hardly have done better under the

circumstances,' he said. 'Your remedies were judicious, and safe.'

'And you find Mr. Penruth's pulse recovering its vitality, I hope?'

'Yes, there is a return of vitality; slow, but palpable.'

'Then I cannot do better than leave him in such good hands,' said Leland quietly. 'Good-night, Mrs. Penruth.'

'Vyvyan,' exclaimed Barbara piteously, seeing her husband's eyes fixed on George Leland with a wrathful look even in their glassy vacancy, 'won't you speak to Major Leland before he goes? Won't you give him one good word for saving your life?'

'Why should I thank him for so questionable a boon?' asked Vyvyan, with faint slow speech. 'It might have been better to let me go. Somebody must have wanted me out of the world very badly.'

'I desire no thanks,' answered Leland. 'I did what I would have done for any *sowar* in my company; no more than I have done for many a cholera-smitten wretch by the wayside. Good-night, Mrs. Penruth.'

Barbara followed him to the door.

'Don't go away,' she pleaded; 'I feel as if we were all safer while you are here. This strange doctor will not stay long, perhaps, and then we shall be alone and helpless again. If Vyvyan has been poisoned, as you think, and as he thinks, there must be a hidden enemy in this house.'

'I believe there is,' said Leland. 'What do you know of that widow, your sister-in-law's maid?'

'Nothing, except that Miss Penruth has a high opinion of her.'

'I have just the opposite idea. And I believe your brother-in-law is of the same way of thinking. I saw him look at her curiously just now.'

'I am full of fears,' said Barbara. 'You will stay, won't you?'

'If you bid me stay, yes. What have I to live for so sweet as to be useful to you?'

'Go down to the drawing-room. I will send my mother and Flossie to take care of you. I shall not leave this room.'

'You are right. Your place is here.'

Barbara went back to the bedside.

'A very sensible person that Major Elam,' said Mr. Fordyce. ' His remedies are perfectly unobjectionable ; in fact so much so, that I shall pursue the same treatment myself, with certain amplifications. You have a nurse, I presume—some trusty old servant who can carry out my instructions ?'

'I will be my husband's only nurse, if you please,' answered Barbara firmly. 'I am quite able to do anything you require done.'

'But you are so young and inexperienced.'

'That is nothing. I have a mind than can learn, I hope ; and I will obey your instructions most faithfully.'

' Very well, my dear young lady, I will not refuse to indulge so natural a desire. I shall not leave Mr. Penruth while his condition is critical. And now tell me, dear madam, have you any idea of any possible manner in which your husband can have accidentally taken poison ? Do you know of any poisonous medicine having been in the house ?'

' No, indeed. There has been no medicine sent for any one since my husband's recovery from a cold and low fever, during which Mr. Didcott attended him.'

'Well, perhaps it may be better to reserve all speculation upon this subject till I see Mr. Didcott. It would be well if Didcott could be here before I leave. Your groom said he was expected to return to his house at Camolet early in the evening. Would it be too much to ask that a messenger might be sent to request him to drive over here at whatever hour he may return?'

'It shall be done,' said Barbara, ringing the bell.

She gave the order to Gilmore, who promised to go herself to the stable and give the message to the right man. Mr. Penruth's dogcart was to be sent over to Camelot, and was to wait there till the surgeon could be brought back.

CHAPTER VI.

LINKS IN THE CHAIN.

MARK went slowly down-stairs through the gathering dusk, scarce knowing where he went, or why he chose one direction more than another. Mrs. Morris had vanished in the darkness of the up-stairs gallery, whether to Priscilla's room or her own Mark knew not. In the hall below all was dusk and silence. The servants, reassured by the coming of the doctor, were at tea in the distant kitchen. The lamps were not yet lighted.

The study-door stood open, and the red firelight within had a cosy look, or would have had to a man disposed to see the comfortable side of things; but for Mark at this moment life was steeped in densest gloom. He felt weighed down beneath such a burden of dread and terror as he had never till now been called upon to bear. The fears that had harassed him when his accounts at the quarries were all wrong, and he lived in hourly dread of detection, were as nothing compared with this awful apprehension of to-day.

Poison : that is to say, secret murder in its basest, most insidious form. Some one, in this honest old house, under the roof-tree that had covered generations of God-fearing single-minded men and women, had been plotting against the master's life, sapping his strength, crushing his spirits, imbuing him with the ever-present fear of sudden death, preparing by slow and gradual measures for the final stroke which was to consummate a murder.

Who was that secret plotter? Who had most interest in making a speedy end of Vyvyan's life? Was it the fair young wife, whose old lover had come back, with fame and honour, ready to pick up the dropped thread of a broken love-story? Surely there could be no one else more likely to desire Vyvyan's death, no one who would profit more; for what can be greater gain than to go back to one's first true love, and be happy?

Mark would willingly have persuaded himself that Barbara was the guilty one; but he could not. The sweet face, in all its tender beauty, rose before his eye,

the face he had **seen** hanging over **his brother's bed,**
like an **angel's, full of pity. No** ; to plot murder
and look thus must be beyond the power of humanity.
Dissimulation may go far, but not to such **a point as**
this. And there had been that other face by the
same bed, a face once passing fair in **his** sight, but
where now he saw the brand of Cain.

And he remembered with infinite horror **that**
night in the cottage on the St. Columb road, when
Lewis Maulford had discussed the younger brother's
chances of inheriting the estate, how those **shrewd**
black eyes had glittered with the rapture of **a greedy**
soul that foresees the accomplishment of **its desire,**
and how the wife of his bosom had **cried, 'If**
Vyvyan were to die ; **if** he were to fall **down in**
a fit !'

The thought of death had been there—thought
and desire too. And then swift on the heels of this
knowledge, acquired from Maulford, had come
Molly's ardent wish to be domesticated at Place ;
that scheme of hers which had seemed to Mark so
foolish and motiveless, but to which **his weaker**
nature had yielded, as it yielded always to her per-

suasive tongue, her kindling eyes, her superior
power of argument, which went so far as to make
the most illogical reasoning appear logical and
sound. He had yielded, angry with himself for
yielding. He had brought his low-born wife into
his brother's house, disguised, falsified, with a false
character. He had done this thing believing that
he was indulging a woman in a foolish whim, the
gratification of which could do no serious harm to
anybody; though it was likely to inflict inconveni-
ence, possibly discredit, upon himself. And now all
his senses were paralysed by the horrible fear that
this seeming caprice was part of a deadly plan; that
Molly had crossed the threshold with the deliberate
intent of shortening his brother's days.

He went into the firelit study, and shut the
door, and sat down on his brother's sofa, which had
been wheeled to the fireside, and thought of all those
facts in the past and present which made the links
in the chain of evidence by which his wife was to be
judged. He remembered her greed of gain; how
she had always harped upon and built upon his
chances of succeeding to his brother's estate; with

what malignant envy she had always regarded Barbara; **how** arrogantly she had asserted **her own** claim, as **the** mother of three brawny boys, against that childless wife. He considered how unlike her natural disposition it was to wish to lower herself to menial offices; she, who had looked **back at** her days of service with such contemptuous self-pity, and had boasted that with the Lanhernes she had been more **like the mistress than the servant.** Yet to gratify this fancy of hers, with no stronger motive **than** a vague idea of acquiring an influence **over** Vyvyan, she had borne with **the caprices** and **petty** tyrannies of a most exacting mistress, she had **subjugated her own** nature, repressed **every feeling,** separated herself for more than half a year from her **children,** left house and home, belied every attribute **of her mind, and to** all seeming **was** no nearer achieving her alleged purpose than she had been the **day she first entered the house.**

And then Mark recollected that the change in his brother's **health** had only come about after Molly had been domiciled at Place. Until this year there **had been no man in** Cornwall hardier or stronger

than Vyvyan. But within three months of Mrs.
Morris's advent the insidious malady had begun, and
the man's whole constitution had changed.

He remembered how he had been attacked in
precisely the same manner after emptying his brother's tankard of home brewed beer. And this
attack had not recurred; there was nothing in the
beat of his heart to-night, even under the agitation
of this horrible fear, to indicate weakness or disease.
Could he doubt that the cause had been in the
draught? that the beer, brewed after the same
recipe for a century and more, had been drugged?

There was the tankard, left on the table after his
brother had taken his last draught out of it—the
draught of triple strength which had been intended
to despatch him; for the murderer, having prepared
every one for the end, and hoodwinked the doctor,
had no motive for delaying the final stroke any longer.
Mark rose and took up the tankard, and lifted the
lid to see if there was any of the beer left. Yes,
there was about a tablespoonful of liquor at the bottom
of the vessel—just enough for analysis, he fancied,
knowing very little about such things.

' If it is she who has done this thing, I will do nothing to help in hiding her guilt,' he said to himself; 'I will not try to shield or to save her. No, though she is my wife, and the mother of my children, I will remember nothing except that she came into my brother's house by stealth, and tried to murder him. Thank God, she has failed : yes, though I were to be a beggar and an outcast for the rest of my life, I can thank God with all my heart that this iniquitous plot has failed.'

He flung himself down upon the sofa, and drew Vyvyan's fur carriage-rug over his shoulders. He lay thus with his eyes closed, not inclined to sleep, but worn out with the agitations of the afternoon, and the turmoil of soul he had suffered since the groom rushed into his office at the quarries to tell him that his brother was dying, and that he must ride his hardest home if he wanted to see him again before he died.

Lying thus, with the fur rug flung over him, Mark's figure was only faintly discernible in the fire-lit room ; not visible at all to the person who crept in presently, with stealthy foot and cautious movements, and stole slowly towards the table where the silver tankard glimmered amidst a confusion of papers, hunting-whips, and hats.

Mark lay with his back to this table, and his face towards a bookcase opposite, an old-fashioned book-case, with a glass door above and drawers below, a bookcase of the period when the average gentleman's library could be shut up in a very small space, and was apt to be kept, like stuffed birds or geological specimens, behind perpetual glass.

The firelight was shining on the glass door, mak-ing it almost as good a reflecting surface as if it had been a mirror, and this reflecting surface showed Mark Penruth the figure of his wife bending over the table, peering into the open tankard.

She moved suddenly towards the fireplace with the tankard in her hand. He guessed that she was going to throw the dregs of the draught into the grate, and sprang up from his sofa to stop her.

Startled by his sudden appearance in a room she had believed empty, Molly drew back with a stifled scream, and let him take the tankard from her hand; but, recovering her self-possession in the next instant, she tried to get it from him.

'What do you want with it?' she asked.   'I was sent here.   I am going to take it to Dickson.'

'Dickson can do without **it** for a few hours.   I **am** going to put this tankard under lock and key.'

CHAPTER VII.

ON A DARK ROAD.

MARK opened a door in the panelling near the fire-place, where there was a roomy closet in which the Squire kept the accumulated rubbish of years—horse-balls and old newspapers, discarded bits and bridles, damaged whips, rusty spurs. Here on a shelf Mark set the silver tankard, and then shut and locked the door upon it, and put the key in his pocket.

'What have you done that for?' asked his wife, confronting him, hideous as a baffled fury, her pallid lips working convulsively, every feature distorted with passion.

That he should rise up against her, this easy-tempered husband, whom she had managed, and bullied, and worked her own will with, during all the years of their married life, was a crushing blow. To meet resistance from so weak a thing was mad-dening.

'Because my brother has been poisoned, and

there may be some trace of the poison in that tankard. I had a drink out of it once, and I know how I felt after that drink.'

'Are you out of your senses as well as the rest of them?' exclaimed Molly contemptuously. 'Your brother is dying of heart-disease. Mr. Didcott knows that. And because he gets delirious and talks about poison, and his wife's lover comes here to echo the cry—more shame to her for inviting him here at such a time—you must take it into your head to be mighty clever and take up the same story. I've no patience with such idiotcy.'

'Come,' said Mark, with a look and manner she had never seen in him before—the look of a man who can be master when his time comes—'don't let us bandy words. I have found you out, woman, and I have done with you. I never knew what it was to be sick or sorry till the evil day you got hold of me. I've never been a happy man since I've known you. But it's all over and done with now. You and I are parted; and if you ever try to set up any claim upon me, I'll do my best to put a rope round your neck.'

'You are a fool!' cried Molly, looking at him with eyes that once had power to make him shiver, but whose angry fire he could defy now he knew the devil's nature that sparkled in them.

'No, I have been an arrant fool, but my eyes are opened. I have sat alone in this room for the last hour, thinking over your wickedness. O you devil! To steal into my brother's house, and try to take his life; so that you might come here and sit in his wife's place, and sleep—you would have slept peacefully, I suppose—in the bed where he now lies at death's door. Come, why should I waste words on you? I know you. That's enough. Come with me.'

'Where?'

'To the hall-door. You have finished your business here, and you've made a mess of it. Please God, my poor brother will live through to-night, and be sound and hale again before he's a month older.'

'You are not going to turn me out of doors, Mark?'

'That is just what I am going to do. You ought

to think yourself lucky if you get off scot-free,
and go and hide your wicked head in another
county.'

This meant, in Mark's idea, remotest exile. A
man who left Cornwall was, as it were, at the Anti-
podes.

'You would turn me out of doors after dark, to
lose myself on the moor?'

'You'll find the road easily enough. Perhaps it
might be the best thing for yourself and others if
you were to get lost. If you stay here much longer
you may have the constables taking you off to
Launceston jail.'

'Who would dare to accuse me?' asked Molly
boldly.

'Facts! Facts which speak pretty plain in this
case.'

'What facts? Who can say that I ever tam-
pered with poison? Who can show that I ever
bought poison?'

'No need to buy the poison that grows in all
our hedges. A few young foxglove leaves were all
you wanted for your work. Will you go quietly, or

shall I tell Dickson to put you out, or send one of
the men for a constable?'

'Do you mean it? Do you mean that you can
stand there, and in cold blood accuse your wife—
your honest wedded wife—of being—'

The white lips faltered. Audacity was this
woman's strong point, but there was a limit even
to her daring.

'A secret poisoner. Yes, that is what I know
you to be.'

'If any one has tried to poison your brother, it
must be his wife. She wants to get rid of him,
that she may go back to her old sweetheart. That
ought to be clear enough even to a fool like you.
Didn't I see those two plotting together a month
ago, and isn't he here now to see how their plot
works? Easy enough for him to find out what the
poison was, when it was he and she that gave it.
I suppose he means to give an extra dose presently,
under pretence of curing your brother. It's a deep-
laid scheme, Mark; but if you weren't a fool you'd
see through it as easy as I can.'

'Are you going, or shall I send for the constable?'

'I am going. If I drop down dead on the way, my death shall lie at your door.'

'Your life has lain at my door, and has been a heavy load for me to bear.'

'You would not shed a tear, I suppose, if you were to hear of my death?'

'Not one. I should thank God for having removed a monster from the earth.'

'My children!' she cried, turning upon him suddenly like a tigress. 'My three bonny boys! What is to become of them?'

'They will be taken care of; you need have no fear for them; they have done no wrong.'

She made no further remonstrance, but watched his face closely as they went across the hall in the lamplight. If she had seen any sign of wavering there, in the face she knew so well, she would have stood her ground and defied this husband of hers, and brazened out the situation to the very end. But she saw in this familiar countenance an unfamiliar look that paralysed her and made her submissive to her own degradation, a look that meant indomitable

will.　For once in his life Mark's manhood asserted
itself, and he was master.

'Do you mean that you and me are to part for
ever like this?' she asked, turning round and facing
him on the threshold.

'God grant I may never see your face again!'

'Will you let me run up-stairs to my room for a
shawl or a cloak?　I shall be frozen to death out on
the moor.'

'I won't trust you out of my sight.　You will be
creeping into my brother's room and giving him another dose.　His life is not safe while you are in the
house.'

'You are on a false scent, as I told you just now,'
she said; 'but it's no use arguing with a madman,
I suppose.　I am not going out on the moor to perish
with cold.　You can go up-stairs with me if you like,
and wait outside my door while I get my shawl.'

He did not wish her to die of cold, any more than
he wished her to die on the gallows.　He only wanted
to get rid of her out of his own life and his brother's,
to make a swift end of her as a source of danger and
woe.　So he just grunted an ungracious assent; and

they went up the back staircase together, to that modest apartment roofed diagonally by a picturesque gable, which had been considered good enough for Miss Penruth's maid.

'Don't be long,' said Mark, as she went into the room.

She was not long. She had made up her mind what she had to do, and did it quickly. She flew to the clumsy old chest of drawers in a corner of the room, unlocked a drawer, and took out a large bottle of a brownish-coloured liquid, labelled Rosemary Hair-wash. She ran to the lattice, opened it, and emptied the contents of the bottle over the ivy which grew thickly up to the window-sill. Then she took a small flat brown-paper parcel from the same drawer, and thrust it into her bosom.

These were all the instruments of a rural Borgia. No casket with spring lock, no retorts, or crucibles, or furnaces, or glass masks, or automatic death-dealing rings had been necessary to her trade. A bunch of leaves and flowers out of the hedges had been all she needed for secret murder.

She snatched a warm jacket from a peg, put on

her close widow's bonnet, and rejoined Mark on the landing.

He led the way down-stairs without a word, she meekly following, till they came to the hall-door. Here Mark stopped to get a coat and hat from the adjacent room where such things were kept.

'I am going as far as the gate with you,' he said grimly. 'I want to see you clear of the premises.'

It was a fine wintry night, planets and constellations shining in the clear cold sky, the moan of distant waves making melancholy music.

Husband and wife walked side by side along the broad gravel road, side by side in unbroken silence, till they came to the lodge. The gates had been shut at dusk, and the lodge-keeper came out to open them, and looked wonderingly at the widow and her companion.

'Good-night,' said Molly, with a last malignant look, when the gate was opened.

'Good-night,' answered her husband; and so they parted, she walking briskly away on the high-road.

'You know that person?' Mark said to the lodge-keeper, when Mrs. Morris's black figure was lost in night and distance.

'Yes, sir; I d' know she well enow. 'Tes Miss Penruth's maid.'

'Miss Penruth has dismissed her. You are not to admit her on any pretence whatever.'

'No, sir, surely. But if she d' come i' the day-time when the gate's open, she'd have nowt to do but walk straight through.'

'You have eyes to see her in the daytime. If she come to this gate, stop her. She has no right on my brother's land. Give her in charge as a tres-passer.'

'Has she been stayling, Mr. Mark, a respectable-lookin' widow like that?'

'Never mind what she has been doing. All you have to do is to keep her off the premises.'

The man shrugged his shoulders and shook his head significantly, as if imagination made up to him in somewise for his ignorance of actual fact.

Molly went her way over the moor, a desperate creature, full to the brim of evil passions and evil wishes; hating every one in the old house yonder,

whose lighted windows made but the faintest glimmer in the distance, when she stopped upon her
lonely road for a minute to hug her jacket closer to
her chest, and to look back at the paradise from
which she had been expelled.

She had made her attempt to win house and fortune for herself and her children, bringing all her
cleverness to bear, plotting and planning with a cool
brain, carrying out her work with an unfaltering
hand, patiently, doggedly proceeding on her dark
road, till the goal seemed close ; and then, swift as a
flash, had come failure and discovery.

She had known from the moment that Indian
soldier entered the room that her chance was lost.
She had felt, rather than seen, his eyes reading her
face, and the secrets of her soul written there. She
hated him almost as intensely as she hated her weak
husband, who had found a will of his own just at the
very crisis when it was vital to her that he should be
blindly submissive.

' I could have held my ground but for Mark's
interference,' she thought ; ' so long as no one in
that house knew who I was, no one had any reason

for suspecting **me**. **But** with that prating fool against
me, I should be ruined. And now what is to become
of me, I wonder? What **have I** got to care about,
or to live for?'

And then, tramping steadily **along the** lonely
moorland road, where you **might walk for** an hour
without meeting **a mortal, this** woman set herself to
argue that question which dilettante philosophers
lounging in Jacobean drawing-rooms, made beautiful
by blue-and-white crockery on sage-green walls, have
lately asked mankind to consider,—is life worth liv-
ing? What was it worth to this baffled plotter, who
had lost the prize for which she had ventured so
deep, and who saw nothing in all her days to come
but disappointment and disgrace? Conscience had
no terrors for her, remorse no sting; in her case the
worm and the **fire were in the sense of** failure; to
have gone so far and succeeded so well, and yet to
have failed at last.

She saw no hope in the future, even if she could
clear herself **in** Mark's sight, and convince him that
she was innocent of the crime with which **he had**
charged her, and win him back again as **a** yielding

and indulgent husband.   What, then, even if this
were possible, which seemed unlikely?   What then?
Mark could not give her Place, or any part of the
wealth that went along with it.   Were he to declare
his marriage he would be a beggar.   He had told
her as much many a time; and now that she had
lived under Vyvyan's roof she was more inclined to
believe in her husband's view of the Squire's character.   He was a hard man; a man not to be moved
from his opinions or his prejudices; capable of generosity, but with an incapacity to pardon.   And if
Mark kept the secret of his low marriage, and the
thread of life were to be taken up again just where it
had been dropped at the cottage on the St. Columb
road?—a decent life enough, surely, for a vagabond
seaman's daughter, a woman who had begun her
career in a low public-house at Devonport, and for
whom the bar at the King's Arms, and the decent
dulness of Camelot, had been promotion.   But for
Molly such a life did not seem worth living.   She
had looked forward to something much better than
this in those summer evenings when she and Mark
Penruth walked in the lanes near Camelot, and her

heart swelled with pride at the thought of her gentleman lover's subjugation. When she married him,
she had **in her** own mind made herself the future
mistress of Place. Vyvyan was a confirmed bachelor,
whose solitary life and eccentric habits made him
appear much older than he was. Vyvyan would be
brought to forgive his brother's foolish marriage—
Molly had an overweening belief in her power over
the sterner sex—and would open the doors of Place
to the bride; and all would go merrily till the kind
elder brother made a peaceful and timely end, and
left Mark and Mary to reign in his stead.

This had been Molly's vision of the future when
the Squire's brother married her. She unfolded her
views to Mark one summer evening as they strolled
on the little sea-walk **at** Sidmouth, at which bewil-
deringly lively watering-place they spent their brief
honeymoon. Mark's very different manner of looking
at things dashed her a little; but she set down his
prognostications to stupidity and cowardice.

'I don't think I'd have married you if I'd **have**
known you were such a poor timid creature,' she said.
'It's all very well to keep things secret for a little

while, and watch your opportunity; but you can't
suppose I'm going to be hid away in holes and corners for ever.'

This was, perhaps, an allusion to certain arrange-
ments which Mark had been suggesting. He was
afraid of taking his young wife too near home, and
had planned a lodging in a back street in Plymouth,
where he might visit her by stealth.

Molly endured the back street in Plymouth and
the rarity of her husband's visits for a twelvemonth;
but at the end of that time she was the mother of a
bouncing boy-baby, and had acquired complete ascend-
ency over the boy's father. She insisted upon his
finding her a home of her own—a home in which she
would have her own furniture and her own servant,
instead of being dependent on the scanty service and
the scantier furniture of a third-rate lodging. She
insisted, further, that the home should be within
easy reach of Mark's office, so that he might devote
his leisure to the cultivation of domestic affections,
and see more of the magnificent boy-baby, and future
inheritor of Place. Mark, after resisting as he always
resisted, yielded as he always yielded, and the cottage

on the St. Columb road happening, just at this time,
to stand empty, seemed to offer a golden opportunity
for establishing Mrs. Mark in a home of her own:
provided always that she would keep the promise she
made before her marriage, and reveal to no living
creature that she was Mark's wife, until he himself
should be prepared to admit the fact and stand by
what he had done. Molly had been ready enough to
make this promise when the chance of her marriage
depended on her readiness so to pledge herself.

The cottage was furnished with goods and chat-
tels chosen by Mary herself, and, for the first year or
so, the pleasure of possessing these chairs and tables,
fenders and fire-irons, with the labour of keeping
the same spotless and shining, satisfied the longings,
and even the ambition, of the so-called Mrs. Peters.
The vision of future glory at Place was always before
her. The cottage was but the purgatory which was
to precede that paradise; but, for a time, the purga-
torial existence was not unendurable. Then came
the weariness of monotony: the chairs and tables,
fenders and fire-irons, were always exactly the same,
polish and scrub as she might; and then there was

the galling sense that the very people who admired her furniture and drank her tea secretly looked down upon her, as a spurious kind of matron, who could give only a garbled account of herself, and had never been known to show her marriage-lines, even to a bosom friend. And out of this weariness and sense of shame there grew an ardent longing to be 'righted,' to have all the praise and glory that was her due as a respectable married woman, whose 'prudence' none could question. Then, when she had borne this dull slow life for nearly ten years, growing more bitter of tongue and snappish of temper every year, came the news of Vyvyan's marriage, to overthrow all her hopes of future greatness. And there and then those seven devils, which lie in wait to take possession of empty houses whence all the virtues and the graces have fled, came and made their abode with Mark's wife, and the vilest thought that ever took shape in a woman's mind was not too vile for her to give it shelter.

It was a long way to Camelot—seven good miles by moor and country road. Yonder, far away to the left, twinkled the lights of Rockport, straggling up the edge of the hill from the harbour in the hollow to the topmost house in the village. Molly thought, with a shiver, of the many cosy firesides in the long **steep** street, of the contented mothers who were sitting beside them—as she might never sit again—with children at their **knees.** **But she had** found little bliss in a cottage and her own fireside. It was **only** now the thing was gone from her that it began to seem sweet. Should she try back, make friends **with** Mark, talk him out of this fancy of his, and begin life again, content to be Mrs. Peters, and to live under a cloud, till Fortune's wheel gave **a new** turn in her favour?

No : she could not go back. On the dark road she travelled there was no turning back. She had failed, and all was over and ended. She had staked all upon this one desperate cast, feeling sure of success.

It was eight o'clock, and all the shops in Camelot were shut, when Molly turned wearily into that up-hill lane where Aunt Jooly had her abode; the merest hovel of cob and thatch adjoining Farmer Somebody's pigsties.

The one lattice—in which there were more paper

and rags than glass—was closely shuttered; but there was a dim glimmer of light shining under the door, so Molly lifted the latch and went in. The room was kitchen, parlour, and bedchamber all in one; Aunt Jooly reserving the upper story, which was far from weather-tight, as a storehouse for apples, onions, and fuel. A bed closely curtained with many-coloured patchwork drapery occupied the warmest corner. An ancient armchair filled nearly half the room, and screened the sibyl from all the winds that blew. An old bureau, in which she kept her simples, and which the country people regarded with awe unutterable, as the repository of mysterious powers, and a rickety little round table comprised the rest of Aunt Jooly's belongings.

A witch would not have been complete without her familiar. Aunt Jooly had two in the orthodox feline form. A twin pair of large black cats adorned and guarded the hearth, and showed an invincible jealousy of the tea-kettle, which they evidently considered a rival in their mistress's affections, and an impediment to their full enjoyment of the fire. These cats had been christened Tom and Jerry, and were as

well known and as much respected in Camelot as the
serviceable Aunt Jooly herself.

The old woman sat over her fire, hidden from
view in the big armchair; but the uplifted counten-
ances of Tom and Jerry, and the black teapot and cup
and saucer on the table, told Molly that the witch was
there. She walked straight to the back of the chair,
and looked down at the old nurse, who was nodding
and mumbling at the cats while she sipped her tea.

'Lord a-mercy!' cried the crone, when Molly
tapped her on the shoulder. 'Who's there?'

She turned round and stared at the face looking
down upon her out of the shadows. Such a ghastly
face, so strange in its expression, that, for the moment, she hardly recognised it.

'Lord, 'tes you!' she cried. 'I thowt you was up
in Lunnon.'

'I have been in London; and now I've come
home, and I want the key,' answered Molly, without
relaxing a muscle in that rigid face. She had drawn
her thick black veil closely round the front of her
bonnet, and tied it under her chin, so as to hide the
widow's cap.

'Lord, but you d' look ill—that white and whist! And all in black, too!' exclaimed Aunt Jooly, staring at Molly, while she fumbled in a capacious pocket for the key. 'There baint nowt wrong with the childer, be theere?'

Molly shook her head impatiently.

'There's your kay,' said the old woman, handing it up over the back of the chair. 'But can't ye come round by the fire and set down a bit, and have a sup o' tay? 'Twill warm you may be, for you look half froze.'

'I've had a cold walk.'

'Why didn't you come in the coach? 'Twas in two hours ago.'

'Good-night,' said Molly, going to the door.

'Well, you're uncommon short with a poor old woman, Mrs. Payters. You'll not find a cobweb in your house, I'll warrant; and 'tes as dry as a bone.'

'Thank you, Aunt Jooly. I sha'n't forget that I'm beholden to you for that,' answered Molly.

She was gone before the old woman could say another word; but Aunt Jooly sat staring at the door for some minutes, to the wonderment, and even uneasiness, of Tom and Jerry, who interrogated her dumbly, by sundry pattings and scratchings of their forepaws on her ancient and bony knees.

'She d' look as if she'd seen a ghost,' muttered the hag.

CHAPTER VIII.

MARK IS WARNED.

WHILE Mark was cutting short Mrs. Morris's period of service, George Leland walked up and down the firelit drawing-room, waiting till he should hear that the patient above-stairs was out of danger, and that Barbara's mind was at ease. He walked slowly up and down the fine old room, which looked its best by this variable light—a light that flashed fitfully upon the bosses and armorial bearings of the richly-carved ceiling, and lent glow and colour to the faded tints of drapery and walls.

He was left for a considerable time with no better company than his own thoughts, and those were not cheering. He had done his duty, but the duty done left no sense of delight. There was none of the rapture, the afterglow which lit his soul at the close of a day's hard fighting—a hair-breadth escape with life and limb where annihilation had seemed inevitable. He had done his duty. Seeing his rival—the man

whom of all men he had most reason **to envy and to**
hate—in the fell grip of death, he had wrestled with
the grim destroyer, as Hercules wrestled for Alcestis,
and had come off victorious. **And now,** alone with
his own thoughts, in cold blood, the battle over, the
victory won, he was able to contemplate what he had
done, and to speculate **upon what** might have happened if he **had** held his hand, stood aside out of the
fray, and left Barbara's husband **to** Fate and local
doctors.

'He was dying,' he said to himself, 'dying of
narcotic **poison**—so nearly gone that **a quarter of**
an hour's delay might have turned the scale. **It**
was not I who poisoned him. Suppose **I had let**
him go—left him to slip into the dark river—should
I have been less a murderer, I wonder—seeing what
I saw, and knowing what **I know—than the** secret
wretch who gave him the poison?'

Conscience told him that his sin would have been
no less than murder.

'Thank God I did not hesitate, even for a second,'
he said **to himself.** 'I had but one thought, one
desire, and **that** was to save him. Now that I have

won him back to life, when he is well again, and he and I are on an equal footing, I may wish him dead; but an hour ago, seeing him helpless, at the last extremity, my soul did not waver. Satan had no power over me.

'Who could have poisoned him, and for what end ?'

This was a question George Leland could not answer, knowing so little of the man's life or surrounding circumstances; but he thought with a shudder how, if Vyvyan Penruth had died by poison, he being in the neighbourhood at the time, suspicion might have pointed to Barbara as the poisoner— might, nay, must inevitably have done so, since the victim had himself accused her.

This would have been the horrible sequence to Vyvyan's death. George Leland trembled when he remembered how near that death had been. Better a thousand times that he and Barbara should be parted for ever than that her future days should be darkened by such a scandal, made loathsome to her by the world's contempt.

He thanked God for the chance that had brought

him to Vyvyan's bedside in time. That flagging pulse, that slowly-labouring heart, whose every **beat** had **grown** weaker as Leland listened, must have stopped before the coming of the Launceston doctor. Vyvyan Penruth would have died in his lethargic sleep, while his kindred stood round his bed, ignorant and helpless.

'That black-eyed woman **was** in it,' thought George Leland. 'I never saw a face that so plainly indicated evil. And she had prevented them giving him brandy, knowing no doubt that brandy was the only thing to save him. Yes, she is the plotter, she is the poisoner. God **knows why.**'

Flossie came fluttering in at this moment.

'No lamp, and the fire almost out, and you have had no dinner!' she exclaimed breathlessly. 'What a horribly rude, inhospitable set of people you must think us! And in Cornwall, too, a county famous **for** its hospitality. Dinner was ready ages ago, but there was no bell rung, on account of Vyvyan, and neither **ma, nor** Miss Penruth, nor I was in the humour to eat anything, so we stayed up-stairs, and Gilmore brought us some tea. But I did suppose

that Dickson would have had the sense to look after
you. I feel perfectly wretched to think you have
been treated so badly.'

'Don't make yourself uncomfortable on my account, Flossie. I don't wish to dine. How is your
brother-in-law ?'

'Better. The Launceston doctor says he will
come all right. It was a sharp attack, but the
Launceston doctor promises to pull him through it.
But it is you we have to thank the most,' added
Flossie ; 'but for you I believe he would have died.
Odd, isn't it ? And wasn't it lucky that I thought
of fetching you ?'

'Most providential.'

'Yes, I generally think of the right thing. I
remembered how you said that if ever Barbara was
in trouble I was to come to you or let you know ;
and here she was in the most dreadful trouble ; and
though I had no idea what you could do to help us,
I felt that your presence would be a safeguard ; so
I bundled on my habit and came.'

'You acted bravely, wisely, splendidly, Flossie.
And now, if the doctor says that Mr. Penruth is out

of danger, I may as well ride back to **Rockport**. I can do no good here.'

'Ride back alone by a strange road this dark **night**?' ejaculated Flossie.

'**It** won't be my first dark ride, Flossie, nor my longest. I have ridden fifty **miles** between sunset and sunrise many a time, and have ridden many a mile by night when I was so tired that I have slept soundly in my saddle.'

'And didn't you tumble off?' asked Flossie.

'Not I! When a man spends half his life on horseback, the movement of his horse is no more than the rocking of **a** baby's cradle. May I ring the bell and order my horse, Flossie?'

'Not till you have dined. I will not let you leave this house without refreshment.'

'Won't you? Well, then, you shall make me a **cup** of tea, and then **I** sha'n't fall asleep as I ride **over** the moor. **Let us drink** tea together, and I'll try to fancy I am in the parlour at Camber-well.'

'Do you remember the first evening?' cried **Flossie,** when she had rung the bell and given her orders. 'I shall never forget how you attacked our bread-and-butter.'

'I had not dined, you see. That was hardly fair in a partial boarder, was it?'

'O, but you made noble amends. York hams and innumerable baskets of strawberries, Dundee marmalade and Scotch shortbread! I wonder we were not all made bilious by your generosity. Those were happy days, weren't they?'

'Very happy,' he answered, with a sigh; and then relapsed into gloom.

Dickson appeared presently with the tea-tray and urn, and Flossie occupied herself in making tea, while George Leland walked slowly up and down the room, almost unconscious of her presence.

In her infinite pity for him, she made his tea desperately strong, and then half drowned it with cream.

'Come,' she said, 'sit down by the fire and be comfortable, as you used to be at Camberwell. And let us talk cheerfully,' she continued, with an assumption of gaiety, when the Major had drawn his chair to the hearth and taken his teacup. 'Tell me about the Mutiny.'

' That is hardly a cheerful subject.'

'No, I suppose it isn't; but it's exciting, at any
rate. You were wounded at Lucknow, **Bab told**
me.'

' Yes, Flossie, badly wounded; as near death as
the most eager experimentalist need wish to be. It
was after the storming, when I had passed scathless
through the breach, shoulder to shoulder with **one**
of the finest soldiers **in** India, that I got **struck**
down by a Sepoy's bullet. I was hunting out **a**
party of ruffians **who were** hiding in the dark rooms
of the Begum's palace, when one of them fired at
me. It was not his luckiest shot, for the High-
landers bayoneted every man **of the** party, while **I**
was being carried off for dead. I was in hospital
three dreary months after this. When my faithful
troopers were told I was killed, not a man of them
believed it. That could not be, they said; Sahib
Leland could not be killed: they had **seen** me so
often come unharmed through the hail of bullets,
and cut my way through a ring of swords without a
scratch. But there must come an end to every
man's career, must there not, Flossie ?'

'Pray don't talk as if yours were ended. You'll go back to India, won't you, by and by?'

'If I live, Flossie; if I live long enough.'

Flossie looked at him uneasily. The hollow cheek, and glassy brightness of the sunken eye, were not indicative of returning health. Major Leland looked weaker and more worn than when she had seen him a few days ago at Rockport. Fired with excitement, face to face with danger, he had seemed all force and power just now by Vyvyan's bed; but the occasion past, and the excitement over, he looked as he had looked in Barbara's eyes that stormy afternoon—a man whose days were numbered.

He would eat nothing, but enjoyed his cup of tea, and told Flossie how often, after a weary ride under the midnight stars, he had longed for that cheering cup, before he lay down to rest in his tent.

His horse had been ordered to be ready for him at eight o'clock. It was now half-past seven.

'You would like to see Barbara before you go, would you not?' asked Flossie.

'No, I won't have her disturbed. She has made up her mind to stay with her husband; she is his safest guardian. But there is some one in this house I want to see—Mr. Penruth's brother. What kind of a fellow is he?'

'Very good-natured,' answered Flossie.

'Does that mean rather stupid?'

'Well, I should hardly call him a wonder of cleverness, but I believe he is a good man of business. He is manager at the quarries, you know.'

'Indeed! Then I suppose he has the average amount of common-sense. I want to have a little serious talk with him before I leave.'

'I'll run and look for him,' said Flossie, 'and ask him to come to you. And then I think I had better go back to poor mother, who is in a dreadful state of mind, and is being made all the worse by that horrid Miss Penruth.'

'That lady does not appear the essence of amiability.'

'She's the sourest, most cantankerous creature! Actually objects to me because I do nothing but read novels, ride her brother's horses, and eat thunder and lightning.'

'Thunder and lightning?'

'Bread-and-treacle and clotted cream,' explained Flossie. 'It's delicious. As if one could do anything better than get rid of time in such a lonely place as this!'

'And how does Barbara dispose of her life?' asked Leland.

'Poor Barbara! She never complains, but her existence must be dreadfully dull when we are not here. And how she can put up with Miss Penruth is more than I can understand. Well, I'll go and hunt for Mark. Good-bye.'

'Good-bye, Flossie. Let me know when you are going home, that I may go to you as soon as you are ready for me.'

'Do you really mean it?'

'Really and truly.'

'I am so glad. We will make you so comfortable,—as our guest, you know; no partial boarding this time.'

'I fear I may be a troublesome guest.'

' How so ?'

' Invalids are apt to give trouble, and I am still on the sick-list.'

' We won't mind that. It shall be our business to cure you. There's a doctor mother had, in a Til-bury,—I believe he's tremendously clever ; and I'm sure he ought to be, for his bill was something frightful.'

' Good-bye, Flossie. Time is going, and I want to see Mr. Mark Penruth.'

Flossie shook hands with him and ran off, with a curious pain in her heart, despite her assumption of cheerfulness.

Mark came into the drawing-room presently, with a pale face and dejected aspect.

' You want to see me, Flossie tells me,' he said.

' Yes; I want to say a few words about your brother's illness before I go,' answered Major Le-land, observant of Mark's pale and anxious coun-tenance.

' I shall be glad to hear anything you can say.'

' You know that Mr. Penruth believes himself to have been poisoned.'

'Yes.'

'I have reason to know that his suspicion is well founded. He has all the symptoms of poison. Now I want to put you on your guard. Medical men are either very slow to find out foul play, or very much disinclined to communicate their suspicions. They leave the coroner to make the discovery when the patient is dead. It's the safer way, for them, and saves trouble.'

'Vyvyan is not going to die.'

'Not from this dose. I want to warn you against a servant in this house. God knows what reason she can have for plotting his death, but I believe that widow woman, your sister's maid, is the poisoner.'

'You need have no further fear of her. She has left this house, never to enter it again.'

'What, then you too had the same suspicion? Mind, I had nothing to go upon but her face. That told the whole story.'

'I had some previous knowledge of her character. Acting upon that, I turned her out of doors.'

'You did wisely, and I believe your brother is

safe. What in Heaven's name could have been the woman's motive?'

'We needn't go into that,' answered Mark moodily. 'She will never come into this house again.'

'It is a blessed deliverance. And now let me recommend you to keep a close watch, and to tell your own doctor everything you know about the attempt that has been made on your brother's life.'

'I shall tell him all that need be told.'

Mark went out to the porch with the Major and saw him mount, and then the two men shook hands and parted, George Leland riding slowly through the mists of a November night.

CHAPTER IX.

A LETTER was brought to Mark early next morning as he sat beside his brother's bed, addressed in a writing which he knew too well. A boy had brought it from Camelot, but had not waited for an answer.

'If you want to see me again,' wrote Molly, 'come to the cottage to-morrow. There are some things that must be settled between us before we part. If you refuse to come it will cause trouble; and as this is the last favour I shall ever ask you, it isn't much for you to grant. You'll find the key of the back door behind the water-butt, in the old place where I used to hide it when I went marketing of an evening.'

Mark turned the letter over and over in his hands as he sat beside the curtained bed, where his brother lay sleeping a quiet and natural sleep.

Yes, he must comply with this request, hateful as it would be to him to look upon the woman's

face again, loathsome as the very thought of her had
become. He **must see her once more, and arrange**
with her **how** her future life was to be spent, and
where. She must not be left without the means of
living, **or** she would commit more crimes, and make
the name of Penruth infamous—that honoured name
which he had been weak enough to give **her.   He**
must provide her with an income, and must make
that income contingent upon her living ever so far
away from Cornwall. **Let her go and hide herself**
in the great wilderness of London, where no one
would know anything about her.

Yes, he must pension her out of his salary, and
he must keep the three boys at school ; pay for their
schooling, and clothe them, and visit them now and
then, and do what he could to compensate them for
the loss of their mother.

' They have her blood in their veins,' he thought
with a shudder. ' What if it should show **itself by**
and by in evil deeds ? Yet they seem honest open-
hearted little fellows now, and they take after my
family in their looks ; they are every inch Penruths.
God grant the bad strain may never show itself !'

He determined to ride over to Camelot in the afternoon, when he had seen Mr. Didcott, and heard his opinion of his patient. Didcott and the Launceston doctor had been closeted together for half an hour last night, and had agreed as to the cause of Vyvyan's illness. Didcott had remained with his patient all night, administering stimulants, and guarding against the possibility of foul play in any quarter. That Vyvyan had been poisoned he was now very sure, but whom to suspect he knew not. Sometimes his thought pointed to Mark, who had so much to gain by his brother's death; and then the needle-point of suspicion veered and turned to the wife, whose loveless marriage-bonds had been so nearly broken.

In any case Mr. Didcott felt that it was his bounden duty to watch the patient. Before he drove away from Place that morning in the chill November daybreak, he took Dickson into his confidence.

'Somebody has been trying to poison your master,' he said. 'God alone knows who it is. I want you to keep watch in Mr. Penruth's room while I am away. Mrs. Penruth is nursing him; that's all very well, but she is young and inexperienced, and wants your help. Don't leave her for so much as half a minute.'

'No, sir,' answered the man, with a troubled look. 'What you tell me is very dreadful, sir. It casts a cloud upon the whole household.'

'No doubt it does, Dickson. It will be somebody's business to find out where that cloud is blackest.'

'It's a curious thing,' murmured the butler. 'I suppose you know all about it. Miss Penruth's maid, sir, a highly respectable widow-person—always seemed rather above her situation, didn't mix and mingle with us, sir, in the 'ousekeeper's room, as she might have been expected to do—'

'Yes, yes, yes, yes—go on, can't you?' cried Didcott impatiently.

'She goes and disappears last evening, sir. No one knows where or wherefore. She had given notice to quit, I allow, but her time wasn't up for another week; and last night she is found to be missing. When ten o'clock struck there was no one to take down Miss Penruth's hair or attend to her little wants. Mrs. Morris's drawers and boxes as usual, but no Mrs. Morris. If the witches had carried her off upon their broomsticks, she could hardly have made a cleaner bolt of it.'

'Strange,' muttered the Camelot surgeon; 'I never quite liked the manner of that woman. I never could get an honest look at her face. She was always hiding in corners, and keeping herself in shadow.'

'If it wasn't unbecoming a Christian and a Primitive Methodist, I should say that I couldn't abide her,' said the butler.

'Well, everything will come out in time, I suppose. Take care of your master; that is what you have to do. He'll be about again in a day or two if all goes well, and then he'll be able to take care of himself.'

Mr. Didcott took his seat in Vyvyan's dog-cart, and rattled away in the damp chilly air, eager to get back to Camelot and settle for his parish patients.

Vyvyan was rallying gradually. Digitalis has the quality, rare among vegetable poisons, of cumulative power, and a long course of digitalis had

brought the strong man very low. Mind and body
had alike suffered; and now, as he lay on his bed,
feeble, almost helpless, his soul was burdened by
the thought that life, won back for him, could give
him nothing worth having.

He still believed, despite Barbara's gentle presence, despite her seeming grief, that it was a wicked
wife's hand which had mixed the poison in his cup;
that it was a false woman's desire to go back to an
old lover which had been the motive for this attempt
at murder. He watched her with dull heavy eyes as
she sat near his bed, or moved softly to and fro to
perform some service for him; watched her in silence
and gloom, believing her a monster of iniquity under
the outward form of innocence and beauty.

He had hardly spoken since his recovery from
the stupor that had lasted so long. Barbara knew
not whether this dumbness was a sign of only half-
recovered consciousness, or whether it indicated an
angry and unpardoning soul. She went on quietly
doing her duty, and made no moan. Sometimes her
thoughts wandered from that dull silent room, and
followed the guest who had been there yesterday—

that dark haggard face, so like and yet so unlike the face whose tender smile had lighted her youth; that gaunt wasted figure, the clothes hanging loosely upon shrunken limbs. O, how changed he was! and yet how familiar and dear his presence had been! and what comfort and security she had felt in the sound of the resolute voice, the fire of the commanding eye!

He had saved her in her hour of need, and now he had gone out of her life for ever. It was not well that they two should meet.

She sat by her husband's bed meekly, patiently, even though there was no look of gratitude or affection in the eyes which followed her every movement when the patient lay awake, watchful in his silence. It was a relief when he fell into a peaceful slumber; and Mark, with the old-fashioned idea that there was something soothing in darkness, drew the heavy damask curtain between the sleeper and winter's brief sunshine.

Dickson had come to help his mistress in her attendance on the invalid. He sat at a respectful distance by the fire, and was ready when there was nourishment or medicine to be given.

Mark stole softly to the window when he had thrust his wife's unwelcome letter in his pocket, and stood there looking at the dark-brown hills rising far off above the level line of the moor.

Mrs. Trevornock and Flossie were taking their rest, after having sat up all night, too anxious to retire till they were told that Mr. Penruth was out of danger. Miss Penruth, reassured as to her brother's condition by the two doctors, had withdrawn to her own room, reluctant to the last, and insisting that her place was by Vyvyan's side. What were the claims of a frivolous young wife, introduced into the family, as it were, yesterday, when weighed against those of a sister who had been born and reared under the same roof?

'I begin to think there is no truth in the saying that blood is thicker than water,' said Priscilla indignantly.

CHAPTER X.

BUSINESS FOR AUNT JOOLY.

Mr. Didcott and Mr. Fordyce, the surgeon from Launceston, met at three o'clock in the afternoon, and pronounced the patient decidedly better; and there and then did the stranger resign all charge of Mr. Penruth to his regular attendant, and accept with due courtesy the handsome fee which Mrs. Penruth slipped into his hand.

'I cannot claim the merit of having saved his life,' said Mr. Fordyce. 'Your friend, Major Selim, was beforehand with me. But for his strong measures, Mr. Penruth would have sunk before I arrived.'

'Thank God he knew how to act !'

'Yes, it is a blessing to have some one with experience and common-sense at hand in such an emergency. A very superior man, evidently. But, tell me, now, Mrs. Penruth,' pursued the doctor, in a confidential voice which neither Mark nor the butler could hear, 'have you any idea how **your** husband happened to take this **poison?**'

'I have no idea; I am utterly in the dark. **He** has no enemy that I know of; he has **done nothing** to provoke **anybody's** enmity; and **yet,** in his own house, surrounded by old servants, **some** one tries to murder him. **It is** most horrible! **It** will make life **a burden** to us.'

'**Surrounded by old** servants, you say, Mrs. Penruth? Then there is no one among the servants whom you could suspect?'

'Why should a servant try to kill him? **For** what motive? There has been only one stranger in the household since my marriage, and that is Miss **Penruth's** maid.'

'She is a respectable person, I suppose?'

'Yes, she was highly recommended. You saw her yesterday. A widow.'

'**Yes, I remember,**' said Mr. Fordyce, who was not a physiognomist; 'a very superior person.'

'Miss Penruth has a high opinion of her. She used **to sit up** with my husband when **he was ill** with low fever a little time ago.'

'O,' said the surgeon, looking thoughtful, ' she
used to sit up with him! Indeed!' And then he
took his leave, pondering as he departed whether
this superior female could be the person who had
dosed Mr. Penruth.

'But what motive?' argued Mr. Fordyce.
'What motive could there be, unless she were only
the tool of somebody else?'

Didcott and Mark were in the adjoining room
discussing the same subject, or rather Didcott
asking questions, and Mark reluctantly answering.

'The thing must be sifted,' said Didcott. 'It
is due to all of us, especially to the members of the
family, that a strict investigation should be made.
The thing has been going on for a long time, you
see; it is a deep-laid plot. I found these symptoms
in your brother nearly three months ago, and took
them for indications of heart-disease, as any other
medical man would have done who knew what I
knew of the family antecedents. The business
must be investigated, Mark, or your brother's life
will not be safe in his own house. I don't want
to make myself troublesome, or to make the matter

public, if it can be helped.   But your brother's life
must be protected.   If it hadn't been for Major
What's-his-name's promptitude, the Squire would be
a dead man to-day.'

'Yes, yes: he shall be protected,' Mark answered, nervously evading the surgeon's eye.

'Do you suspect anybody in the house!'

'Well, yes; I had my suspicions last night,
considering the various circumstances of the case.
The person I suspect is now out of the house.'

'I understand.   It was that shifty-eyed widow,
your sister's maid.   I never liked her.   Then it
was you who sent her away ?'

'Yes; but you needn't say anything about it to
my sister.'

'But what motive could she have had ?'

Mark tapped his forehead significantly.

'You think she was queer in her head, eh ?   It
was a curious form for madness to take, though.
Never knew a case of the kind.   Homicidal mania
generally shows itself in violence ; but a slow, cautious, sustained attempt at poisoning is hardly
compatible with insanity.   Your lunatic is never

capable of consecutive action. He forgets to-day
what he did yesterday.'

'I can't account for the thing in any other way,'
said Mark moodily.

'I can't account for it at all,' retorted Didcott;
'but it must be accounted for. Such an attempt
mustn't pass unquestioned.'

He went back to his gig, which had brought him
over from Camelot, and drove home, sorely troubled
in mind. He began to fear that his suspicions of
yesterday were but too correct, and that his old friend
Mark must be concerned in this diabolical attempt;
in which case the mysterious widow was doubtless
Mark's accomplice, and had been made the scape-
goat. Who would profit so largely as Mark by
Vyvyan's death? The surgeon remembered how
they had talked together of the Squire's fatal malady,
and how Mark's eye had brightened as he spoke of
the horses and hounds he would keep when he became master at Place.

Mark waited till Mr. Didcott had been on his
road for half an hour, and then went out to the
stable to get the brown cob saddled, and on that

unamiable brute started at **a** thundering trot for Camelot. It was dusk before he rode along the quiet road where stood the stone cottage in which **he had tasted the joys** and cares of surreptitious domesticity.

There was no cheerful glow of fire or lighted lattice to guide him to the spot; but he knew every inch of the ground, even in this misty duskiness of winter evening, and he led the cob round to the back of the premises, and tied him to the post of a low wooden gate which opened from a ploughed field into the little kitchen-garden behind the house. The back windows, like the front, were all dark.

Mark tried the back-door, and found it locked.

' She's out, evidently. Why did she ask me to come if she was going to be gadding about?' Mark interrogated inwardly, as he felt for the key in its hiding-place behind the water-butt.

His heart sank within him with a sharp and bitter pang as he remembered many a home-coming in the past, when his wife and her small servant had gone on some household errand, and he had **let** himself in quietly, and had sat by the firelit hearth waiting patiently for Molly's return; pleased if she came home bright and good-tempered, and seemed glad to see him; forbearing even when she was snappish and reproachful.

She had been his wife, the woman of his choice, perfectly beautiful in his sight, the mother of his bonny boys; and he could not contemplate her wickedness without the keenest anguish.

He went to this meeting of to-night with reluctance and fear. He knew his wife's power over him, how she had always been able to argue him into a surrender of his own opinion, and a tame submission to her will. He had been able to stand against her last night, for horror and wrath had made him iron. But should he be able to stand as firm to-night? Might not her tears or her passionate assertion of innocence beat down and overrule his own conviction of her guilt? Could he, who but once in his life had mastered her, and that by the force of supreme indignation, master her again in his cooler temper of to-night?

'Let me think how she tried to kill my brother, how she would have made me an unconscious accomplice in his murder,' he said to himself, as he opened the door.

Within, all was dark and dreary. It seemed strange that there should be no gleam of firelight on this winter night. He went into the kitchen, which smelt of damp, and groped about for candle and matches. Having found these and lighted his candle, **he went** into the parlour and looked about him. All was empty, dull, and cheerless; the neat little room, once so snug and bright upon winter evenings, had the aspect **of** a place which has been long uninhabited. Mark's heart sank as he looked at the hearth where he had so often romped **with his** boys, tossing and tumbling them over and over like a litter of puppies, in the rosy firelight. He had not **been** happy beside that fire, for discontent and discord had been the sauce to his meat, and the bitter in his cup, from **almost the beginning** of things; but there were some sweet memories, nevertheless— childish kisses, childish laughter, chubby arms entwined about his neck.

He sat beside the cheerless hearth and waited, wrapped in gloomiest thought. **The** minutes were

intolerably long. He expected momently to hear
the click of Molly's key in the front-door, and he
started at every crack of the furniture, at every
creak of the leafless branches outside the window.
He waited for half an hour, and then began to get
uneasy, and to think that his wicked wife had played
him a trick. He was very uncomfortable about his
horse, which he had left shelterless in the cold.

'I had better have put him up at the King's
Arms,' he thought; 'but I didn't want any one to
know I was here.'

Too impatient to sit still any longer in that deserted room, Mark took up the candle and went on a
voyage of discovery, to see if by chance a letter had
been left for him somewhere to inform him that Mrs.
Peters had changed her mind, and left Camelot without waiting to see him.

He looked into the other parlour, but there was
no letter. He went up the narrow staircase to the
principal bedroom, which it had been Molly's delight
to keep a picture of neatness.

One glance at the white curtained bed showed
him a figure lying there, and he called—forgetting

for the moment all that had happened—'Molly!' in the old familiar tone. A second glance froze the blood in his veins, and he went slowly up to the bed, and shudderingly touched the icy hand, and bent down to look at the awful face.

It was his wife, dressed in the black gown she wore when she left Place—dead. A mug, with a little brownish liquid at the bottom of it, stood on a table near at hand. This, Mark fancied, had held the sleeping draught which lulled her to that last long sleep.

What should he do? He sank into a chair, helpless, paralysed with horror. Slowly his power to think and act came back to him.

'I must do something; I must tell somebody,' he thought. 'I can't sit here alone all night—looking at her.'

Then, wiping the cold sweat from his forehead, he rose and moved towards the door, leaving the candle where he had put it down. He would not leave his dead wife alone in the dark.

'I'll fetch Didcott,' he said to himself, hurrying out to his horse. 'He has always been my friend.

I must tell him everything. And the nurse, old Aunt Jooly, she can be trusted; those two between them can do all that's wanted.'

He mounted the cob and rode down the hill to the High-street, where Didcott's lighted surgery window gave him a feeling of comfort. The surgeon was drinking tea, and eating squab-pie, after his drive from Place, and was telling Mrs. Didcott the state of affairs in the Penruth mansion. He came out at Mark's summons, profoundly astonished.

'Your brother no worse, I hope,' he cried. 'There's been no relapse, eh?'

'No; I came away half an hour after you. I want you, badly, up the road, yonder.'

'At the cottage?' asked Didcott. 'Why, there's nobody living there, is there?'

'Don't I say you are wanted? Come this instant! I'm going to fetch Aunt Jooly; but I shall be there before you.'

'Well, upon my soul, now that's rather hard upon a poor beggar,' grumbled the surgeon, who had been making up medicines in his senna-scented surgery for the last hour, and had only just settled to his comfortable meat-tea. 'Aunt Jooly, **too**? **It must** be another baby. **They might have given me notice.**'

'**Shall** I put the pie **in the** oven?' asked Mrs. Didcott.

'Not a bit of use. Goodness knows how long I may be away.'

Mark hurried on to Aunt Jooly's hovel, and, finding the witch at home, **bade her come to** the cottage instantly. She too speculated upon a baby, **and made a** bundle of her night-gear and sundry other **necessaries** before she **started**, and looked in at a neighbour's to confide **Tom** and Jerry to friendly **care, so that those** familiar **spirits should be** nourished and provided for in the event of her prolonged absence.

Didcott found Mark waiting for him at the cottage-door.

'**What is it?**' he asked. 'Anything bad?'

'Very bad,' answered **Mark**: 'she's dead, and I believe she has poisoned herself.'

'My God!'

'Didcott, **I** had better tell you all **the** truth, **at** once,' said Mark, grasping him by the arm, as they stood in the dark passage together. 'She was my wife. I kept our marriage a secret because I was afraid of offending my brother.'

'I suspected as much all along,' answered Didcott.

'That isn't all, though. Six months ago she took it into her head—when my sister wanted a maid —to go to Place, under a false name, with a false character. I opposed the plan, tooth and nail; but she would have her own way. It seemed a foolish fancy; but there was no particular harm in it, as I thought, and I gave way.'

'Then she was the woman they called Morris!'

'Yes.'

'Now I understand why she always fought so shy of me. I could never get a look at her face. And now she has poisoned herself?'

'I'm afraid so.'

'After trying to poison your brother. It's a bad business, Mark. First and last, I don't think I ever heard of anything worse. How do I know you were not in it?'

'You know me,' said Mark, with a touch of manly

feeling; 'that ought to be answer enough to your question.'

'Well, old fellow, I believe you,' replied the surgeon. 'But I have been very uneasy in my mind, I can tell you, since last night. I've always taken you for a good-natured fellow, who would go out of his way rather than tread upon a worm; and to think that you had a hand in poisoning your brother—it was a fearful thought! Well, you've got yourself into a confounded mess, and I must see you through it. There'll have to be an inquest, I'm afraid.'

'Can't that be avoided somehow?'

'I think not. It will be best to do things in a regular way, and bear the brunt of it. Very little need come out, beyond the circumstances of her death. I think it will be wise for you to come forward and state that she was your wife. Everybody in Camelot knows she was associated with you; there's no hiding that; and it will be safest to tell the truth. If the fact of the marriage were to come out afterwards, it would be awkward for you.'

'I'll do what you like. But it will ruin me with my brother. I shall have lost everything.'

'Who knows? He may not be so hard upon you as you think.'

'He has been softer-hearted and kinder to me since his illness. Well, I must brave it out,' said Mark.

Didcott went up-stairs to the bedroom. Mark waited at the open door for Aunt Jooly, who presently arrived, breathless, and hugging her bundle. Mark briefly told her that it was for the dead, and not for the newly-born, her services were needed, and bade her go up-stairs. She went, groaning and bemoaning at every step.

'The handsomest woman in Camelot,' she sighed, 'and as good a friend to me as I ever had. I saw it in her face last night. She was that white and whisht!'

CHAPTER XI.

DEARER THAN MONEY.

THE inquest was held next day at the King's Arms; and the coroner and twelve jurymen—most of whom had known Mark's wife years ago, when she was the smartest and briskest of barmaids, and when sharp retorts and impertinent sallies fell from her cherry lips as readily as the pearls and diamonds shed by the fortunate damsel in the fairy tale—went in solemn conclave to look upon her dead face in the darkened cottage-chamber.

Mark told his story briefly: how the deceased woman was his wife, and he had kept his marriage concealed on account of his brother; how she had been away for some time, and had returned without notice, and had sent him a note which brought him to the cottage, where he had found her dead.

At the coroner's request Mark showed his wife's last letter, which told nothing more than he had said.

'You have quarrelled, I conclude from this,' said the coroner, when he had read the letter aloud to the jury.

'Yes, we had quarrelled.'

'Seriously?'

'Yes.'

'And you contemplated parting?'

'Yes.'

Mr. Didcott stated that the deceased had been dead for some hours when Mark summoned him to her. He would say that she had been dead ten hours. The cause of death was no doubt an overdose of an infusion of foxglove, the dregs of which had been found in a mug close by the bed. He had made a microscopic examination of these dregs, and had discovered seeds, and traces of leaves in the liquid. He had been shown a pipkin, which had been found on the kitchen hearth, containing the pulpy remains of leaves and flowers from which the infusion had evidently been made. This infusion might have been taken ignorantly as a sleeping draught by a person unacquainted with its power. This opinion had an effect on the jury, who, taking into consideration that the Penruths were one of the best families in North Cornwall, and that a verdict of *felo de se* would be an uncomfortable blot upon the family history, were unanimously of opinion that the said Mary Penruth had died accidentally from the effect of an overdose of sleeping stuff; taking her departure out of this life as innocently as a babe which is launched into eternity by an injudicious dose of comforting syrup.

Mark breathed more freely when it was all over, and his old friends were standing round him in the inn-parlour, murmuring consolatory speeches, and shaking hands with him in a kindly and protecting way.

'And now I must go and make a clean breast of it to my brother,' he said, cutting short all friendly manifestations, 'before he gets well enough to read an account of to-day's business in the newspaper.'

He lingered only to arrange with Didcott about the funeral. The family surgeon was to see to everything. It was to be a quiet respectable funeral, in the little churchyard yonder among the fields. Would Mark follow? Yes; it would

be best, perhaps, to silence scandal. He and
Didcott would go together in a mourning-coach:
that was all.

Mark rode slowly homeward, pondering on the
difficulties that still had to be faced. Yet though
those difficulties weighed heavily upon him, there
was a sense of relief which in his mind seemed to
lighten all his troubles. For ten years his wife had
been his one abiding vexation. She had embittered
every day of his life, and during the last forty-eight
hours her existence had been a horror to him. She
was gone. He looked back at his life with her
shudderingly, as a man might who had lived un-
awares cheek-by-jowl with a cobra.

Mark had spent the previous night at Camelot,
but Didcott had been to Place early in the morning,
and had brought back a good account of Vyvyan's
progress. He was going on slowly towards recovery,
but he was wonderfully silent and low-spirited.

'You can't conceive how this business has
shaken him,' said Didcott; 'he looks ten years
older since it began. It was touch and go that
night, I can tell you.'

Mark put up his horse, and then went straight to his brother's room. Vyvyan was sitting in the big armchair by the fire, watching the burning logs, with dull hopeless eyes. He had always been gaunt and bony, but he looked now a mere shadow of the once vigorous Squire. Barbara sat on the opposite side of the hearth, with a dainty little table before her, and some delicate fancy work in her hands. She too was pale and sad, and it seemed as if all the brightness of her youth had departed for ever.

Vyvyan acknowledged his brother's entrance with a nod, but did not even look up.

'Well, old fellow,' said Mark, with an attempt at cheerfulness, 'ever so much better, I hear. Worlds better, isn't he, Barbara?'

'Yes, he is much better, Mr. Didcott says. He will soon be well, and able to go for a drive on the moor. Am I to drive you in the pony-carriage, Vyvyan, or will you go in the landau?' asked Barbara, looking up from her work with tender deprecating eyes, as of one who sued for pardon, yet hardly knew how she had offended.

'It doesn't much matter which,' answered Vyvyan.

'I shall be in the way in either vehicle, I daresay.'

The gentle eyes looked up at him again, and
seemed to ask, 'How have I deserved this?' But
Barbara's lips made no answer.

'Where have you been, and what is the matter
with you?' asked Vyvyan, looking at his brother,
who had come to the front of the hearth, and was
standing there with the light full on his face. 'You
look as if there were something wrong.'

'There has been something very wrong. I have
been in great trouble. I should like to tell you all
about it, Vyvyan, even though it may make you
angry—set you against me for ever, perhaps.'

Barbara had risen instinctively, and was gathering up her work.

'I had better leave you together,' she said.

'Yes, dear; I shall be glad if you will leave us
alone for a little while,' answered Mark. 'Is there
anything Vyvyan ought to take during the next half
hour—wine—medicine?'

'No, there is nothing. I shall be in the dressing-room. Call me when you have done talking.'

And so she left them, looking back anxiously at Vyvyan's moody face as she crossed the threshold, fearful lest there should be some angry discussion between the brothers; for although not a Christian of Miss Penruth's lofty type, she was by nature a peacemaker.

Mark seated himself in Barbara's chair. Vyvyan had relapsed into moody silence, and seemed hardly conscious of his brother's presence.

'You feel better, don't you, Vyvyan?' asked Mark presently.

'Yes, I suppose I am better. There has been no return of those horrible sensations.'

'Are you not glad to know that the idea of heart-disease was a false alarm?'

Vyvyan looked up suddenly, the dull eyes kindling, the stern lips quivering with pain and anger.

'Glad to know that I have been poisoned in my own house? Glad to know that secret murder has been sitting at my hearth—smiling in my face? Glad to know that I have been meshed in a web of treachery and fair-faced wickedness? Glad— Great God! Do not talk to me, Mark. Leave me to fight my battle alone—to work out my life in my own way.'

'Vyvyan, you have some horrible suspicion! You are wrong, utterly wrong! Vyvyan, brother, forgive me, if you can! It was I that brought your enemy into the house, not knowing her wickedness. I know who it was that tried to poison you. I know all about it. Didcott knows it too. He can bear me out. It was my wife.'

'Your wife! What wife?'

Mark told him the whole story—the story of his weak yielding to temptation fourteen years ago, and of all the evil that had come of that folly and his concealment of it. Vyvyan listened with fast-beating heart, with the glow of new-born gladness kindling on his hollow cheek.

What was it to him that his life had been attempted, that a secret foe had been in his household, if that secret enemy was not the wife of his bosom, the idol of his later life? His soul thrilled within him as he heard Mark's confession. Forgive his brother's folly, forgive the weakness of mind and purpose which had so nearly brought him to the grave! Yes, he could forgive anything now that he knew his young wife was innocent, pure, and **perfect** as he had always thought her till that vile letter was **put** into his hands.

He covered his face and wept aloud—tears of mingled remorse and joy.

' I thought it was my **wife who** wanted to shorten my days,' he said. ' That thought made the coming back to life more bitter than death itself. God **for**-give me! **Yes, I** thought it was Barbara's work!'

' **O** Vyvyan, how could you? God gave you an angel **for a** wife, and yet you could not trust her!'

The brothers clasped hands.

'I have been an arrant fool,' said Mark. ' Can you forgive me—a fool, and not always an honest **one? You** may as well know all the truth. **I had been** robbing you for the last three **years** when Maulford came to make out that balance-sheet. I had been unlucky on the turf, and had speculated **in** mining shares, in the hope of getting back what I had lost, and had muddled away thousands of your money. **If** Maulford hadn't doctored **the** accounts, you must have known all about it. I've been an **honest** man since then, **upon my soul, I** have! I

pulled up short, and haven't wronged you of a sixpence—'

'Curse your sixpences!' cried Vyvyan, rising
feebly out of his big chair. 'There is something
in this life dearer than money.'

He went to the dressing-room door and called
'Barbara!'

He opened his arms as she came towards him,
and took her to his breast.

'My dearest love, I have wronged you,' he murmured, with unspeakable tenderness. 'I know all
now.'

She answered not a word; and looking down at
her blanching face, her husband saw that she had
fainted in his arms. Half an hour afterwards he
knew a secret that promised the fulfilment of his
fondest wish, a hope that had almost left him. He
was not to die childless; he was not to be the last
of the good old line. Before the earliest leaflets of
spring were unfolded he might be a father.

CHAPTER XII.

CLEARING THE ATMOSPHERE.

FROM that day forward there was a new tenderness in Vyvyan's manner to his wife. It seemed as if he could not be kind enough, could not be considerate enough, to make up for the great wrong his thoughts had done her. The man's whole nature seemed to be changed by the ordeal through which he had passed. It was as if he had begun a new life. He was kinder even to Mark than of old, despite that confession which showed how very low his brother had sunk in folly and sin.

He called Mark into his study one day, and told him of the hope that shone before him in the immediate future, like a planet which beams so near the edge of earth's horizon that it seems to belong to us more than all the other stars.

'With God's grace, there will be an heir or an heiress to this estate before next year is three months old, Mark,' said Vyvyan; 'so you see I have been obliged to alter my will. I had given up all hope of children when I put you in for the land, and I thought my days were numbered. It's only fair I should tell you of the change.'

'You are very good,' said Mark, stifling a sigh. 'Of course I knew that will was made under exceptional circumstances. I never expected it to stand— after—after we had found out that Didcott was wrong about your heart. Thank God that you have a good old age before you. I am more than content, so long as you leave me in my old berth at the quarries. And it's very good of you not to have pitched me out neck and crop, Vyvyan, after what I told you the other day.'

'No, Mark, I am not going to turn you out. The quarries will be yours when I am gone. I have put you in for those instead of the land. Priscilla has plenty. Take care of the business, and don't get into any more muddles with your accounts. You may feel all the more interest in nursing the property now that you know it will be your own by and by.'

'Vyvyan, you are a good fellow !' Mark exclaimed rapturously. 'An out-and-out brick ! And I am glad there is **going to be an** heir. Yes, heartily, honestly glad. And if you would only start a dozen **couple** of harriers next season, **I** don't think **I** should **have** anything left to wish for.'

' Wouldn't you, Mark? Well, I'll think about **the** harriers. But there are those boys of yours— my nephews,' said Vyvyan, making **a wry face; for** he could not forget their detestable maternal parentage just yet awhile. 'I—I hope they're [not like their mother.'

' Not a bit. They are every inch Penruths.'

' I'm glad of that. **And they are** at school at St. Columb, you say? Poor little creatures! **Where** will they spend their Christmas **holidays ?'**

' At school, I suppose.'

' That seems hard, with their uncle's big half-empty house **so near.** Bring them **over for a** week or so, and let me see what they are made of.'

' **O Vyvyan, that is kind of you!** I am sure **you** will like **them.** They are **such** jolly little beggars, **and** as strong as fox-hound puppies.'

' Let them come, they will do **me** no harm.'

Christmas was close **at** hand, and Mrs. Trevor-

nock and Flossie had been invited to remain at
Place for that social season. They were to return to
Camberwell in the first week of the new year, when
Flossie was to dance at a grand ball at one of the
stuccoed palaces on Denmark Hill. Early in the
new year, too, Major Leland was to take up his abode
with them; and, exquisitely as the house in South-
lane was always kept, there would be much sweeping
and garnishing necessary, in Mrs. Trevornock's
opinion, before things could be meet for his recep-
tion. She had already discussed with Flossie the
desirability of a mahogany wardrobe with a plate-glass
door, in place of the old-fashioned chest of drawers
which now adorned the 'large airy bedroom' that had
been offered to the competition of partial boarders
five years ago. She had serious thoughts, too, of a
new carpet, and something more fashionable in wash-
stands than the existing arrangement in japanned
deal.

The mother was very happy in the new hopefulness which brightened domestic life at Place.
Barbara was glad, with a subdued gladness, always
tempered with sorrow; for it was ever in her mind

that before her there lay a great grief, as well as a strange untasted joy. There was to be loss as well as gain. The resolute eyes that had shone upon her in her darkest night of trouble, the strong hand that had helped her, were never to be near her again. It was in vain that Mrs. Trevornock and Flossie talked hopefully of the balmy spring days in which Major Leland was to regain health and strength, and be nursed and pampered out of all his ailments. Barbara had never forgotten her first impression when she looked into his face in the gray autumn light and saw the stamp of death there.

He had left Rockport, and was staying in Somersetshire with his sisters. A brief note to Mrs. Trevornock had announced his change of address.

About a week before Christmas, Miss Penruth called her brother aside one morning, after breakfast, and announced that she had accepted an invitation to spend the sacred and mildly festive season at Plymouth.

'I ought to have gone much earlier,' she said, ' for there has been a course of Advent sermons that I should have rejoiced to hear ; but I did not care to

leave till you were out of danger, much as I value the
opportunities which Plymouth affords.'

'That was very kind of you,' answered Vyvyan
civilly. 'But as there are such—opportunities, I
think you said—in Plymouth, don't you think it
would be better if you were to live there altogether,
with an occasional friendly visit here, of course, to
maintain family feeling?'

'Vyvyan, am I to understand that you wish to get
rid of me?'

'I don't want to put it offensively. But the fact
is, you and Barbara have never cottoned to each other.
You don't seem to like her. I don't know why, or
ask why. The fact speaks for itself. And then you
have such a rooted objection to her sister, who is a
good-natured, inoffensive little thing.'

'Inoffensive!' screamed Priscilla. 'Her flippancy
would not be abashed by an archbishop. I see,
Vyvyan,—I understand what has taken place. I have
been undermined.'

'My dear Priscilla!'

'I have been undermined, and I had better go.
I am not a pauper to whom bed and board can be a

matter of moment. I have an income which is more
than adequate to my wants, and I have friends; yes,
I thank Providence, I have friends who will gladly
receive me, and will know how to value me.'

And thus, without a word more, it became a settled thing that Miss Penruth should depart. There
was no quarrelling; no disputation, vacillation, she
would and she would not, in the whole affair. She
saw that her brother meant her to go, and she had
too exalted a sense of her own dignity to run the risk
of being told his meaning a second time. So Mark
the sinner stayed, and Priscilla the saint departed;
and every one was pleased.

Vyvyan's health and spirits mended rapidly after
that understanding with his wife. He was a new
man, and took new delight in old familiar things.
He looked back at the days when he sat by the fire
brooding upon sad fancies, and waiting for death.
Life seemed all the sweeter for that dark memory.

'Death must come sooner or later to all of us,'
he said to himself; 'but it was a freezing thought to
think that he was standing on the threshold of my
door.'

He went so far as to write a brief letter to Major Leland, thanking him for the promptitude that had saved his life; and this he showed to Barbara before it was posted.

'I don't want him to think me ungrateful,' he said; 'for I know he acted nobly. He might have let me die like a dog if he had chosen. I doubt if I should have been as generous in his place.'

'I do not believe you would have acted ungenerously,' his wife said, with her grave trusting look.

She had been told just so much as was necessary of Mark's story; and she, her husband, Mark, and the two doctors were the only people who ever knew the history of the crime by which Vyvyan had so nearly lost his life. The gossip that followed the inquest flagged and dwindled and gradually died away, and the scandal of Mark's foolish marriage became only a legend of Camelot life, a tale for Aunt Jooly to tell to future generations.

Priscilla devoted herself for about a week to the task of packing up her belongings, which were numerous; and then, after a sour leave-taking of brothers and sister-in-law, she went her way, only to reënter the house as a visitor.

'I don't think you'll often be troubled with me, Vyvyan,' she said, drawing her slim figure to its utmost height, as she stood on the threshold by the Squire's side, while her lighter luggage was being stowed into the carriage. The bulk of her possessions had gone before in one of the farm wagons.

'You will be welcome whenever you please to come, Pris, so long as you come in a friendly spirit,' answered Vyvyan, touched by that kindly feeling which is apt to soften a man's heart when he is getting rid of a troublesome relative.

'You cannot want me, Vyvyan,' retorted Miss Penruth, in her severest voice. 'Don't let there be any pretending between us. You have new relations whose presence here has been made a perpetual insult to me. I leave the field open to those new relations. I yield to those new claims; and I hope—yes—whatever I may feel as a woman, as a Christian I hope that the course you have taken may result in your happiness.'

She emphasised this speech with a deprecating

shrug and a pensive elevation of her eyebrows, which
implied that her fears were stronger than her hopes,
gave her brother a frosty kiss, and then mounted the
landau with an air of melancholy dignity which must
have been equal to Madame Roland's ascent of the
scaffold. Vyvyan watched the carriage as it drove
away, but he was rewarded by no backward look from
his sister. She sat with her face towards Launceston, and her back resolutely turned upon the home
of her childhood.

'In a better world I shall be better appreciated
and better understood,' she said to herself; '*there* I
may find my proper level.'

CHAPTER XIII.

A NEW GENERATION.

CHRISTMAS came, and the three sturdy boys from St. Columb, red-nosed and red-eared after a journey outside the coach, in their father's care, arrived one frosty afternoon at Place. Mark had written to the schoolmistress to tell her that the boys were motherless; and that worthy person had, with due caution, informed her three pupils that their mother was in heaven—a fact which they accepted with singular equanimity, proceeding forthwith to inquire where they should spend their holidays. Not a tear was shed, till the eldest boy, inspired with a sudden terror, burst out into a lugubrious howl, and asked if his papa had gone to heaven too.

'We couldn't do without pa,' he said; 'pa used to tell us about Jack the Giant-killer, and play with us by the fire, and take us for rides round the field on his horse, and give us pennies.'

Loud was their delight when the father arrived

one bleak windy morning, and announced that he was going to take them home for a week's holiday.

'Who minds the house and scolds Lucy, pa, now that ma's in heaven?' asked Jack, the eldest boy, when they were all three in their perch behind the coachman, Mark occupying the box-seat in front of them.

'You are not going to the cottage, Jack. That's shut up till somebody else wants to live there. You are going to a big house on the moors, ever so big.'

'Is that the house ma used to talk about when she was angry?' inquired Jack, who was of the little-pitcher age, and had tolerably long ears. 'The house she called Place?'

'Hush,' whispered Mark, putting up a warning finger, and with a side glance at the coachman, whose face had no more expression than a dead wall, but who might have been listening to that shrill small voice all the same. 'You mustn't talk about your mother.'

'Why not? She's in heaven, Miss Powle says. Heaven is a nice place, isn't it?'

'Yes, yes.'

'Nicer than St. Columb?'

'**Ever so much nicer.**'

'**And St.** Columb is nicer than Camelot. We shall all go to heaven one day, Miss Powle says, and **then** we shall see ma again. I hope she won't scold us as much as she did at the cottage, and that we sha'n't have cold meat **so often.** Will there be washing-days **in heaven?**'

'**No, no.** You mustn't say such things, Jack.'

'**I'm** glad there'll be no washing-days, for **we** always had cold meat when there was washing.'

'**You** are going **to** a house where you'll have hot meat every day,' said Mark, patting the chubby cheeks; 'but you mustn't talk so much about your dinner. It sounds greedy.'

'I am greedy,' replied the little lad, with edifying candour. 'Everybody says so. I sold my comforter to Billy Blake for a wortleberry pasty. Miss Powle said I was as bad as Esau—you know what Esau did, don't you, pa?—but she said Billy was a mean boy, and she made him give me back the comforter. I couldn't give him back the pasty, for I'd eaten it, so I got the best of **the bargain. Did God** make Jacob give back Esau's birthright? If Billy was mean, Jacob was mean too, wasn't he?' argued the lad.

'You mustn't argue about your Bible, Jack. You must read it and ask no questions.'

'Ah, but there's a book we learn out of—*Bible Questions*. So you see you may ask questions about the Bible.'

'Proper questions, of course, Jack—such as are printed in books. Those may be asked. But you mustn't mix up Billy Blake and Jacob. That's wicked.'

'O,' said Jack, gravely acquiescent, 'then I'll read the Bible, and try not to think about what I've read, for fear I should mix up things.'

The first effect of the fine old Tudor house upon these youthful spirits was to awe and subdue them. They were dumb when Barbara welcomed them; they had not a word for Mrs. Trevornock or Flossie. They bit their thumbs—not in the defiant manner of Shakespeare's Sampson, but in absolute bewilderment of mind. They went about from room to room, clinging to their father's coat-tails, and gazing open-eyed and open-mouthed at the faded splendours which were to their unaccustomed eyes as solemnly grand as the vaulted aisles of a cathedral. They explored the stables, under the same paternal guidance, and timidly patted the sleek necks of unknown horses, and made acquaintance with strange dogs, one of which acknowledged their juvenile attentions by an inward rattling sound of an alarming character, as if his whole internal economy were convulsed by wrath too deep to find utterance in vulgar barking.

But by the time the little lads had been two hours at Place, and had been refreshed with meat and drink, this salutary awe wore off, and left them bolder than brass. They had already discovered that the old oak bannister-rail was a capital thing for sliding upon, and were making alternate descents, amidst peals of shrill laughter, when Vyvyan came in from his ride.

The sound of that childish mirth, the cluster of rosy cheeks in the dusky hall, moved him strangely. He felt no anger at this profanation of the quiet old house, only a thrill of sweetest hope. His children's laughter would be sounding thus, some day, he

thought; his children's bright faces would greet him
when he came home. O happy welcome, O sweet
smiling future, which made all life seem new!

'Well, my little chaps,' he called out, with gruff
good-nature, 'let's have a look at you!'

The laughter was hushed at the sight of this
grim stranger. The boy in the act of sliding put
the break on, and descended slowly, his eyes rounded
in a solemn stare. The other two stood still at the
foot of the old brown staircase.

'So you are all Penruths?' said Vyvyan, prod-
ding Jack's red cheek with his bony finger.

'Yes; pa says we are to be called Penruth now.
Our name was Peters till to-day. Ma was Mrs. Peters, but she's in heaven.'

'You mustn't talk of your mother here,' said
Vyvyan, frowning.

'That's what pa told us,' said Jack. 'Is heaven
a wicked place?'

'Heaven wicked—no!'

'O,' said Jack, looking puzzled, 'I thought perhaps it was a bad place, and that it was wicked of ma to
go there, and that was why we mustn't talk about her.'

Phil, the second boy, and Harry, the baby, looked on open-eyed at this encounter, staring up at the tall gaunt uncle, and wondering who he was. Their father had told them a good deal about this unknown uncle, and had warned them how they were to behave to him: how they were not to chatter impudently, but only to answer when he spoke to them; for he was a very particular man, and was not used to children. And here was that irrepressible Jack arguing with this particular man on terms of equality! Phil, the prudent, gave him a nudge, and whispered that perhaps the strange gentleman was their uncle.

Vyvyan's quick ear caught the word.

'Yes, number two,' he said, looking down at the upturned wondering face, 'I'm your uncle, sure enough. And what's your name, my little man?'

'Philip.'

'And yours, number three?'

'Harry.'

'Good old family names, both of them; and you are Jack, I suppose, whom your father thinks such a philosopher. Well, Masters Jack, Phil, and Harry, welcome to Place. **Make yourselves** as happy as you can, in a quiet way.'

'Were we being noisy when you came in?' asked Jack.

'Well, yes, there was a considerable riot.'

'Miss Powle lets us make as much noise as that in recreation time, and says nothing. But we have to be quiet at our lessons.'

'We make faces, though,' said Harry, who could hardly speak plain, 'and we pinch each other under the table.'

'What a big house this is!' exclaimed Jack, staring round him at the twilit hall, the panelled walls, and stags' heads, and armour. 'Is it yours?'

'Yes, it is mine, so long as I live to own it.'

'Why isn't it pa's as well as yours?' asked Jack. 'Brothers ought to share everything. Miss Powle says so when we have apples given us.'

'Miss Powle doesn't belong to the landed gentry, or she wouldn't talk nonsense,' answered the uncle.

'What's landed gentry?'

'Jack,' cried Phil, 'pa said you were not to ask questions.'

'You seem fond of your father, young ones,' said
Vyvyan.

'Yes, we all love pa. Pa's always kind. Ma was
cross—sometimes.'

'Very offen,' said the baby.

'Only on washing-days—or when we tore our
clothes,' said Phil deprecatingly. 'Jack, you know
ma's in heaven, and it's rude to talk about her. If
you don't mind us sliding down the bannisters, uncle,
we'll go on playing.'

'I think,' said Vyvyan gravely, 'that bannisters
which were made in Cromwell's time were never
meant to be slid upon. Besides which you might
break your necks. Come with me, youngsters, and
I'll find some one to amuse you.'

He marched the boys off to the drawing-room,
where Barbara and her mother were talking together
in the deep embrasure of a window, while Mark and
Flossie played draughts at a little table near the fire;
Flossie rabidly eager for kings, and dashing through
the enemy's ranks with reckless gallantry, which
generally resulted in the wholesale slaughter of her
men.

'What do you mean by abandoning these poor little chaps to their own devices?' asked Vyvyan, coming to his own particular chair by the fire, while Barbara rose to greet him with that gentle reverence for his graver age which seemed more the manner of a dutiful daughter than a wife.

He bent down to kiss the pale thoughtful brow.

'Yes, dear, ever so much better for my ride,' he answered to her murmured inquiry. 'The moorland air will soon blow back the old strength. And you, darling,—what have you and your mother been doing all the afternoon?'

'We've been so amused with the little boys,' replied Mrs. Trevornock, 'and their surprise at the house. It is quite a pleasure to hear their young voices ; and it makes one think—'

'Of a day when there may be the sound of still younger voices,' said Vyvyan. 'Yes, I thought of that when I heard their laughter.'

'Do you think they are like the family?' asked Mark timidly, as if it were audacious to make such a suggestion.

'Yes; I can see a look of my father in those young faces—a curious half-comic likeness—the face of middle age hinted at in the rosy cheeks and blue eyes of the child. Yes, they are genuine Penruths, Mark; and we must take care they are brought up so as to do honour to the good old name.'

The three boys stood in a row before the fire, gravely allowing themselves to be roasted, rather than offend the particular uncle by too much locomotion. Flossie, seeing how stupid and helpless they looked, and perceiving that complete annihilation would be the lot of her men, or ever she was able to crown one of them, was moved to pity the children.

'Come and have a romp in the picture-gallery,' she said, 'and then you shall have some tea. I think I'll give you the game, Mark, if you've no objection.'

'I think you've lost it,' retorted Mark, laughing; and then he went off with them for a game at hide-and-seek in the long gallery, out of which the bed-rooms opened.

From that time forward Flossie was the children's prime favourite. They liked Barbara, who was always gentle and tender to them, but whose face had a look of settled sadness which kept them aloof. They loved Mrs. Trevornock, who had a pleasant way of loading their plates with all the most bilious things on the table, and who saved platefuls of dessert to carry up to their room and administer to them at bedtime, whereby they went to bed in a sticky and semi-glutinous state, their cheeks and chins smeared with preserved ginger and other confectionery, and fell asleep with their mouths full of macaroons; but they positively idolised Flossie, who romped with them and told them stories, and gloried in all their most mischievous tricks, and was more impish in her ways than any of them.

'There isn't a boy at Miss Powle's equal to you,' said Jack. 'How I wish you went to school there! Wouldn't she go on at you!'

'Do you think I should lead her a life, Jack?' asked Flossie, pleased at this compliment.

'I believe you'd send her daft,' said Jack. 'She cocks her bonnet up at the back so high that some folks say **she isn't** quite right in her head; but **if** she had you to worry her she'd cock it higher, and then they'd put her in Bodmin Asylum.'

'Wouldn't that be fun?' asked Harry, with juvenile hard-heartedness.

'Well, come **now,** she might **be a worse** old woman,' remonstrated Phil, '**though the** plums in our Wednesday pudding are almost **too far off to** halloo to **each** other.'

'I've christened it beetle-pudding,' said Jack; 'for it **looks more like a lump of dough in which** half **a** dozen black-beetles had gone astray than a genuine plum-pudding.'

'You shall have a genuine plum-pudding to-morrow,' said Flossie—'such a pudding, such a turkey, such mince-pies! **How** dreadfully ill you will all be next day!'

'**It's worth being ill** for **once in a way, if one** can have one's fill of Christmas pudding,' retorted that young sensualist Jack. 'Mrs. Gilmore's making the pudding now. I ran into the kitchen and saw her at it, and we're all to give it **a** stir before we go to bed to-night, **for luck.'**

'Ma never let us stir the pudding,' said Phil.
'She used to be cross on Christmas-eve because pa
wasn't with us. Sometimes Aunt Jooly used to
come and bring us nuts and tell us stories; but we
never had much fun.'

CHAPTER XIV.

SWEETER THAN MARRIAGE BELLS.

CHRISTMAS had come and gone, and the new year had begun. Mark's three boys were back at school. They had departed regretfully from a land overflowing with treacle and clotted cream, otherwise thunder and lightning, but not wholly unblest; for Gilmore, the old housekeeper, had packed for them such a hamper as only the luckiest boys take back to school; and Flossie had driven them down to the lodge where the St. Columb coach was to pick them up, and had stuffed their pockets with sweetmeats; and what with tips from Vyvyan and Barbara and Mrs. Trevornock, they had departed, as it were, in a shower of half-crowns. Mark went back with them, having certain explanations to make to Miss Powle, who had known her pupils hitherto by the name of Peters, and who was henceforth to cherish and honour them as Penruths.

A day or two after the little boys left, Mrs. Tre-

vornock and her younger daughter set off on their
long wintry journey, Flossie elated at the idea of seeing shop-windows again.

'How I shall enjoy a walk down Regent-street, if
I can but get that lazy mother of mine to go with
me!' she said. 'Even the Road will be lovely. I
wonder whether the fashions will have changed since
we left Camberwell! One thing was settled before we
came away; a crinoline is indispensable. Mine is
only a weak invention of the dressmaker. I must
get a real one directly I go back.'

'You will be kind to him, won't you, mother
darling?' said Barbara, when she and her mother
were having their last five minutes' loving talk together in her dressing-room, Mrs. Trevornock
wrapped up to the chin in her daughter's Christmas
gift of sables.

'Kind to him, Barbara!' ejaculated the mother,
whose thoughts were full of an approaching event,
and who had made up her mind that the coming
stranger was to be a boy. 'Kind to your baby!
Why, I shall worship him!'

'No, mamma dear; you don't understand,' said

Barbara, pale and grave to sadness. 'I was speaking
of Major Leland. He is to be with you next week,
Flossie says; and he has so much need of care and
kindness.'

'My dear child, I will do everything—everything
that affection can do to make up to him for all he
lost in losing you. But, O my love, I am so thankful to God things happened as they did! To have
had you in India during that fearful time! I never
went to bed at night after reading of those agonising
scenes without thanking God you were not there. It
might have been, Barbara. You might have been
sacrificed, like so many brave true-hearted wives, and
innocent unconscious children. God has been very
good to me.'

'And you will be good to him, mother—to him
who avenged those innocent victims, who held his
own life as nothing, and who, I fear, has lost it. I
saw death in his face,' she said, stifling a sob; 'and
I should like to think that his last days were spent
peacefully with you and Flossie, and in the garden
where we were so happy. And, mother, if he were
dying, and wished to see me again—as he might

perhaps—I would come at that sad hour—come at
any hazard—to hold his hand at the last—hear his
last sigh.'

'You would not disobey your husband, dear.
He has been so good.'

'Yes, he is good; he has a noble heart.   I
believe he would let me come.'

'You mustn't give way to such sorrowful ideas,
pet,' urged Mrs. Trevornock soothingly.   'Major
Leland is going to get well and strong again, and to
go back to India and be made a General of the Sud-
der Dewanee,' she added, having vague ideas of
Indian distinction, derived from half-heard descrip-
tions of places and people, dimly comprehended by a
mind troubled, like Martha's, about many things.
'We are going to give him the strongest beef-tea,
and calves'-foot jelly, and eggs beaten up in sherry,
and I know we shall cure him of all the mischief
done by that dreadful bullet.   So you must be cheerful, dearest, and only think of pleasant things.'

'The carriage is waiting, if you please, ma'am,'
announced Gilmore; and Mrs. Trevornock, who
knew that the coach would not wait more than five

minutes even for people of distinction, blessed and
embraced her daughter, gathered up handbag, um-
brella, cloak, and other oddments, and, aided by
Gilmore, conveyed herself down-stairs to the hall,
where Flossie was talking to Vyvyan and Mark in
quite a family party.

It was a hard thing for Mrs. Trevornock to leave
her daughter just at this time, but Barbara had so
set her heart upon the carrying out of Flossie's
scheme with regard to Major Leland, that the mother was fain to give way.

'He needs you more than I can, mother,' she
had whispered. 'God will take care of me.'

They were gone, and the old mansion seemed
painfully silent without Flossie's rippling laughter,
and the rustle of her silk flounces, and the air of
movement and brightness which one frivolous young
woman was able to impart to life in a quiet country
house. But even in its stillness, in the gray winter
days, Place was a happier home than it had been
before calamity so nearly wrecked it. Barbara and
her husband were more united than they had ever
been—united by a hope and an expectancy which

filled the mind of both. Vyvyan's grave tenderness
would have won grateful affection from a more stub-
born heart than Barbara's. She had seen him dying,
as she believed, the victim of a mysterious doom; she
had held him in her arms when the death-damps
were gathering on his brow; had watched beside
him as he came slowly back to life; and in those
awful hours she had counted over the sum of his
goodness to her.

'If he should die and never know that I am
grateful to him!' she said to herself at that time.
And again: 'What have I ever done to prove my
gratitude?'

And now he was well again, quite the old Vyvyan,
a rough-hewn figure, a rugged face; but that stern
countenance was made beautiful by eyes that could
kindle with tenderness when they looked at the fair
young wife on the verge of womanhood's great ordeal.
How deep was that love when, one March midnight,
after he had been pacing the long gallery for hours
with muffled feet, noiseless save for the loud beating
of his heart, Didcott's familiar voice called him to
his wife's dressing-room, and, in the rosy firelight, in

a cradle festooned with soft snowy drapery, Vyvyan
Penruth saw the round pink face of his first-born,
and a pair of luminous eyes, more beautiful than he
had supposed it possible for human eyes to be, looking boldly up at him. A being which had no existence an hour ago was here to claim and hold his own
as Penruth of Place. The distant bells rang out
across the windy sky while the father still stood at
gaze, wondering that so fair a creature could be
mortal, and still more that it could belong to him.
Mark had ridden off through the darkness to set the
bells ringing by ringers forewarned and ready; Mark
had shown honest hearty joy at the birth of the
heir.

This was the beginning of a new stage in Barbara's existence. It was almost as if the old purposeless life, so empty of real happiness, had been
blotted out, and she had entered a world where all
things were new. The vanished gladness of her
youth was renewed to her in this innocent young
life; the future, so dim and formless before, took
shape and meaning. The future meant Baby Vyvyan, and Baby Vyvyan's joys and sorrows, failures

and triumphs. The young mother's thoughts, which a little while ago had been so dull and stagnant, went rippling gaily down the river of years to the far-away point where the widening stream of boyhood runs into the broad ocean of mature life. She had something to hope for, something to dream of, in the days that were to come. All her being, all her power to love and suffer, to hope and rejoice, was not to be buried with the old lover, whose life was slowly, but surely, ebbing to its dark close, far off in the old familiar home.

Yes, George Leland's days were numbered, and the number of them was dwindling to a point. Barbara had heard of him from her mother and Flossie very constantly since he had been an inmate of the house in South-lane. Sometimes the letters had been full of hopefulness; the dark shadow of impending doom had been lifted for a little while, and all was sunshine. Major Leland had been wonderfully well; he had walked up and down the pathway by the hazels for an hour, enjoying his cigar. He had gone with Flossie for a stroll in the Walworth-road, and had bought her some lovely gloves, and had made

fun of the bonnets in Mrs. Jones's window; and he
had eaten with more appetite during the last few
days, and had declared that Mrs. Trevornock's mock-
turtle soup was nicer than the real turtle at the Go-
vernor-General's table.

'He is very happy with us,' Flossie wrote in her
last letter. 'He never goes to London, to his clubs.
He is not strong enough to face the east winds; and
we seem to have nothing but east winds nowadays.
Some of his club friends have been down to see him,
men who were through the Mutiny, and it has been
quite delightful to her them talk of their adventures.
One young ensign was evidently struck with *me.*
They are all indignant about the Delhi prize-money,
of which nobody has yet received sixpence; though
the treasures of ever so many native jewellers, who
had hidden their property when the Sepoys got possession of the city, were dug up after the siege—
uncut sapphires and rubies and cat's-eyes—wouldn't
you delight in being the owner of a fine cat's-eye, so
distinguished, you know?—gems of untold value.
Shawls too, and embroidery of gorgeous colours, vel-
vet, silk. It makes one's mouth water to hear about

such things.   But these brave devoted soldiers are
to have nothing.   To hear of such injustice is enough
to make one turn Radical, and insist upon the five
points of the Charter, though you know, dear, that I
am a stanch Conservative, and have always considered Radical opinions the essence of vulgarity.'

Then had come other letters, sad in tone, which
told of failing strength, sleepless nights, days of pain
and restlessness.

'A celebrated London doctor came down to see
him yesterday,' wrote Mrs. Trevornock.   'It was at
his sister's wish, to please his people in Somersetshire; for he is quite satisfied himself with Mr. Asplatt, the gentleman who attended me, and whom
you may remember.'

Might remember!   Poor Barbara!   Could she
ever forget those dreary days of her mother's illness,
which had made an epoch in her life, the days in
which she had brought herself calmly to face the
greatest sacrifice a child can make to filial duty, the
sacrifice of a woman's fealty to her love.

'He is perfectly satisfied with Mr. Asplatt, who
is most attentive, but on his sister's account he gave

way and sent for Dr. Styles, whom Mr. Asplatt recommended as the great authority on this particular complaint. Dr. Styles and Mr. Asplatt saw him together, and had a long talk afterwards in the next room, and then Mr. Asplatt told me Dr. Styles's opinion. You have asked me to hide nothing from you, darling, to tell you the actual truth, however cruel that truth may be, and I feel it my sad duty to obey you. The doctors have no hope, dearest. Everything is being done that can be done; but a long period of exposure and privation, severest fatigue, heat and cold, has had a fatal effect on Major Leland's constitution. The bullet which pierced his chest at Lucknow he might have recovered from, terrible as the wound was, for the lungs were untouched; but the suffering he had undergone previously had sapped his strength, and there was no power of complete recovery. The voyage home prolonged his life, but the seeds of disease were deeply rooted, and neither rest nor medicine could restore the strength he wasted so recklessly in the weary days of the Mutiny. He may linger for weeks, or even months, but he will never be well again. He

knows this, dear, and waits for the end with beautiful resignation.   I cannot tell you how dear he has
grown to Flossie and me in this sad time, and what
a consolation it has been to us to nurse and care for
him.   His sisters were anxious to come to him, but
he wrote to beg them not.   He had wished them all
good-bye when he was in Somersetshire, he told
them, and for them to meet again would be only to
prolong sorrow.'

This letter arrived towards the end of April, when
Vyvyan the younger was just four weeks old, and
when the window in Barbara's dressing-room was all
abloom with spring flowers; the colours and perfume of which were supposed to have already engaged the infant's attention, and to have set his
budding faculties in motion.   If he opened his eyes
a little wider than usual he was supposed to be 'taking notice;' a feeble smile was accepted as evidence
of profound thought; a chuckle was taken for a
burst of wit; so fondly did mother and father watch
for the dawn of reason.   On this fair April day,
when all things had a happy look, Barbara sat by
the window robed in white, pale as a saint in an old

Flemish picture, the baby lying in her lap, and her mother's letter in her hand.

Vyvyan the elder came in while she was reading it.

'How sad your face is!' he said. 'I hope there is no bad news in your letter?'

'Only news I have been expecting for a long time,' she answered quietly, handing him the letter as she spoke.

He read it from the first line to the last with a face that was full of thought, but not of anger. Twice he glanced from the letter to his wife, as she sat looking up at him with sorrowful eyes and parted lips.

'Would it make you happier to see him again before he dies? Would it be any comfort to you to bid him good-bye?' he asked.

'Vyvyan, how did **you know**, how could **you** guess? That is the favour I wanted to ask you.'

'I could read as much in your face. Well, I will be no churl to him at the last, though he was happier than I in winning your love.'

'My first love, Vyvyan,' she said gently, giving him her hand.

'What! Is there a second version of the same story? Is it possible for a woman to love twice?'

'I have learned to love you,' she answered. 'I think I have been stony-hearted and slow to win, but your patient goodness has conquered even my cold heart. Do you despise my love, Vyvyan, because it has come so late?'

'Despise your love, my treasure, my delight!' he cried, kneeling by her side. 'If a rough-hewn fellow like me could find words to express idolatry, I would tell you the value I set upon your love. I have been your faithful slave, Barbara, from the hour I first saw you. I should have been your slave to the last, had you treated me ever so badly. And now, dear, if you are very sure that it will be a consolation to you to see Major Leland once more— remember how full of pain such partings are—we will go to London as soon as you are strong enough to travel. I owe him some recompense, poor fellow; for I fear I was sadly wanting in gratitude that night when he dragged this weary body and soul of mine out of the jaws of death. I thought life such a worthless boon just then that I resented his impertinence in forcing the gift upon me. Now, now that life is worth having, I can afford to thank him for his pluck and readiness.'

So it was settled between husband and wife, without further discussion, that they should go to London and spend a week or two at a West-end hotel, so soon as Barbara should feel capable of taking such a journey. Gilmore, who had been promoted to the office of nurse, and who believed that no such infant as Vyvyan Penruth had ever yet adorned the earth by his presence, was to accompany her mistress in charge of that wonderful baby.

'Vyvyan,' said Barbara, looking up at him with earnest eyes when this journey had been decided, ' there is nothing you have ever done for me—and you have loaded me with benefits—which has so proved to me the goodness of your heart as this act of to-day.'

CHAPTER XV.

THE FORTUNE OF WAR.

In these glad spring days, the season of Proserpine's rough wooing, when the borders were glorious with yellow daffodils, George Leland was just able to creep slowly up and down the garden-walk, leaning on his stout bamboo-cane, and sheltered from east winds by the vine-clad wall—just able to travel at slowest pace, stopping every now and then to take breath, from one end of that half-acre pleasure-ground to the other. To these narrow bounds had he come at last; he who, a year and a half ago, thought it a trifle to ride seventy miles between dawn and midnight; he who had been first among the young athletes at Shrewsbury. It had come to this: two roods of garden at a halting pace in the midday sun; and for all the rest of his day the dull confinement of a sick-room, and for his nights sleeplessness or harrowing dreams.

He knew that he was to die, and he had resigned

himself long ago to his fate—had, indeed, taught
himself to think that death was better than life,
since he had so little to leave or to lose.   Yet there
were times when the old fire flashed from his dark
eyes, when his heart beat loud and fast at the vision
of what might have remained for him to do had life
been longer; most of all at the thought of his
native regiment, the wild hillmen, soldiers of his
own making, who, when they joined him at Delhi
after long severance, pressed round him and leapt
about him like a pack of foxhounds round a beloved
master, kissing his hands and feet, his bridle, his
stirrup-leathers.   With those faithful fellows he
had done some wonderful things in the plain before
Delhi, where his very name had been a terror to
the foe.

He had cut his way to fame and honour with his
sword.   Money he had never valued, and twelve
years' unparalleled work had brought him but little
of this world's gear or gain.   He had flattered no
patron, cringed to no authority, military or civil.
Through the dark cloud of an unmerited disgrace he
had come steadily to the front; and had been, for

his age and standing, one of the foremost men in India when a Sepoy's bullet, fired from a dark corner of a deserted palace, made a sudden end of a career that had promised so much.

'Fortune of war,' he said to himself, as he lay on the sofa where he and Barbara had sat side by side, bending over Hindostanee exercises or playing chess, in the happy days that were gone. Ah, what games at chess those were, when lovely eyes lifted shyly to his made him forget to castle just at that critical moment in which castling meant victory; or when the tremulous touch of a little hand checkmated him more completely than queen and bishop, knight and pawn. Such vile playing, such happy players! It was all over. The Crimean war had been fought; the great Sepoy rebellion had smouldered and blazed, and had been extinguished, not without glory, not without loss, and Church and State were rejoicing at the restoration of peace in that far away empire. Cabinets had gone out and come in; everybody was growing old and gray and grave: the story of life was over, and here came death with the last chapter.

He was a wonderfully patient invalid, **though his** disease was one in which death does not come **pain-** lessly. He **had** hours of suffering, hours of ease. **The** first he bore with silence, and troubled no one with his pain. In his easy hours he was almost the George Leland of old; and Flossie, **who was** his constant nurse **and** companion, sometimes found herself forgetting **how** swiftly the dark end was bearing down **upon them.** **If** he was patient **and** resigned, his **young** nurse was heroic also after her own fashion; **for when her** heart was sorest, she contrived to be cheerful.

'What good you do me, little Flossie!' **George** Leland said to her one sunny morning as they were slowly pacing the narrow walk, his lean brown hand resting on her shoulder. 'How could **I** have borne these **slow** hours of decay without you?'

'You would have had your sisters,' said Flossie, blushing at his praise.

'They are very good, and would have been skil- **ful** nurses, I daresay; but they would **not have** reminded me of Barbara, they do not belong to the happiest time **of my** life, as you do. You seem part

of a bygone happiness, Flossie; a link in the chain
of that golden past, which I brood upon and dream
about now when earth's future lies within such
narrow limits. Men whose days are numbered love
to dwell upon the past. Memory serves them instead of hope. No, Flossie, my sisters could never
be to me what you are. Even the house in which
this body of mine was born is not so dear to me as
the house where my heart found its first and only
mistress. That was a second birth which counts
for more than the first. Then, again, my sisters,
all but Marian, have other interests — husband,
children. Even Marian has her Sunday-school and
all the poor of the parish under her protection. She
could never be such a companion to me as you
have been.'

'I am so glad,' faltered Flossie. 'I only wish
you were going to be with us always.'

'To turn your house into a hospital for incur-
ables,' said Major Leland, with a smile half sad, half
tender. 'You are generous enough even for that, I
believe. If I had come back from India a truncated
creature, the mere hulk of a man, yet in excellent

health, and warranted to live to eighty, you would
have taken me in and cherished my poor carcass, and
devoted yourself to making life tolerable to a lump
of infirmity.   Happily, my love, the complaint I
suffer from is not without a cure.'

Flossie looked at him interrogatively, with tearful eyes.

'Death, dear, the sovereign remedy for all dis-
eases.   Don't cry, my pet.   If—if—I could see her
again, just once more look into those lovely eyes, feel
the touch of that gentle hand, I think I could say
with Manfred,

     " 'Tis not so terrible to die."'

'You shall see her; she shall come to you!'
cried Flossie.   'I will write to her to-day.'

'Not for the world!' cried George Leland.   'She
has a new care, a new love—her son!   If she would
leave her husband to come to me, she would not leave
her son.'

'She shall leave all the world, for your sake; just
to see you once more, just to clasp your hand.   She
told mother she would come if you asked for her;
and you have asked, and she shall come.'

'She shall come, for the end is drawing near,'
thought Flossie full of sadness.

Every morning, let the sun shine ever so brightly,
or the air be ever so balmy, she could see how the
little walk across two roods of ground cost the sick
man a sharper effort; how the hollow cheek grew
hollower, and the unnatural lustre of the eye less like
the brightness of health.

CHAPTER XVI.

RED CLOTH AND OLIVE-LEAVES.

They had made up a bed for Major Leland in the garden-parlour, and had thrown open the folding-doors between the two rooms. His complaint was one in which fresh air was essential, and Mrs. Trevornock gladly sacrificed the daily order of her house to his comfort. She and Flossie could be anywhere, she said naïvely, when the invalid protested against this usurpation of the two sitting-rooms. The kitchen was quite good enough for them to take their meals in.

'Indeed, we are very fond of the kitchen,' said Flossie. 'In the old days we used to sit there sometimes, for pleasure, when Amelia had an evening out.'

The 'old days' meant the time before Mrs. Trevornock's income was supplemented by three hundred a year from Cornwall. There had been certain improvements and alterations in the little domicile

since this expansion of means, which leant rather to
ceremony and refinement than to actual homely
comfort; and Flossie sometimes alluded with a sigh
to that less wealthy period of her life, when it had
seemed a natural thing for her to sit in the kitchen.

It was the beginning of May, and weather fairer
than May often brings—sunshine as warm as early
June. Flossie had found one adventurous lily of the
valley unfolding its waxen petals in the shady angle
of the wall, and had brought it triumphantly to the
Major, who lay on his sofa by the open window, and
fancied to-day that his two roods of pathway would
be almost an impossible journey.

'A little later, dear,' he said, when Flossie pro-
posed their usual walk. 'I know it is the loveliest
morning we have had yet. The blackbird in his
wicker cage next door has been telling me so re-
peatedly since sunrise; but I hardly feel equal to my
constitutional just yet.'

'Do you see this?' asked Flossie, holding up the
lily.

'Barbara's favourite flower! Yes; I remember,
the first night we drank tea together in this room,

there was a bunch of lilies of the valley on the table, and you two girls had each a cluster of the same flower in your belts. You were yourselves as fair and pure as lilies, and I fancied I had come into a world of flowers and simple innocent things. How happy we were that evening!'

'Happy!' echoed Flossie. 'I can't make out how it was ever in us to be so ridiculously happy. But you see, after growing up almost strangers to masculine society, it was something stupendous to find ourselves with an officer actually our own pro-perty. For you seemed quite to belong to us by the time we had finished tea.'

'When I am dead, Flossie,' said George Leland, who had been looking dreamily out of the window while the girl talked, 'I should like some one who has cared for me a little to lay a bunch of lilies of the valley in my coffin. Will you do it?'

'Don't talk like that,' cried Flossie, bursting into tears. 'They will be out of season long before then.'

'I doubt it, dear. I think that the lilies and I may go out of season together.'

Two days ago she had talked of writing to her
sister. Nothing had been said about Barbara since
then. George Leland had asked no question of his
devoted nurse; but more than once she had seen his
eyes resting interrogatively upon her face, she had
marked a nervous expectation in his manner when
there was knocking or ringing at the front door.

'Let me read you to sleep,' said Flossie, grieved
at his restlessness on this particular morning.

Nothing seemed to interest or amuse him. His
books, his papers, were looked at and flung aside.
His attention evidently wandered all the time she
talked to him. Mrs. Trevornock's kind face, looking
in at the door now and then to see how he was going
on, did not win from him the usual smile, the usual
friendly greeting. His thoughts were astray. He
was even fretful and impatient—he who had never
before been so since the beginning of his illness.

'Let me read you to sleep,' repeated Flossie,
opening a volume of Byron. 'You generally do fall
asleep when I read poetry. I am very glad of it, for
it's good for you, though it's not a compliment to
my reading.'

'Very well, dear. Half an hour's sleep would be a boon. My thoughts and fancies would not let me sleep last night, and the blackbird kept me awake this morning.'

'That blackbird must **be** murdered, or sent away,' said Flossie. 'I know you like the *Giaour*, don't you?'

'Infinitely.'

'Perhaps you prefer the *Corsair*.'

'No, let us **have the** *Giaour*. The gentleman's moral character **may be** open to question, but he knew how to love.'

'We'll skip the description **of Greece,' said** Flossie, with whom worship of nature was not a strong point, 'and come to the pith of the story.'

And then she began, 'Who thundering comes on blackest steed?' and warmed with her subject. As she went on, her cheeks glowed and her eyes kindled, and she read just a little less vilely than the average schoolgirl.

George Leland loved his Byron. In that wild hill-life of his, in many a lonely night under canvas, with the covering of his tent **drawn** back to admit the glow of the fire outside, and no prospect but the black sky, or the visage of an occasional jackall, or a possible tiger, peering at him across the flames, he had sat in the red light reading one of the few books he could contrive to carry about with him in his nomadic life. The want of many books had been a trouble to him in his rare intervals of leisure; and his half dozen volumes, Shakespeare, Byron, Shelley, Plutarch, *Don Quixote*, and the Bible, had grown all the dearer to him because they formed the beginning and the end of his library.

He knew that passionate tale by heart, and could have repeated it more fluently than Flossie read. He lay listening with half-closed eyes. The wild horse-man, the reckless rider, the skilled swordsman, the true lover, yes, here was a hero, faulty, no doubt, but with whom George Leland could sympathise. As a sedative nothing could have been better than Flossie's reading. She had a strong sense of the swing in the verse, and she gave a gentle up and down accent to the metre, like the lapping of sum-mer wavelets against a sea-wall, or the drip, drip of a fountain.

The invalid had had a bad night; and after listening lazily for a little while his chin sank upon his breast, and a gentle refreshing sleep stole over him just as the insect queen of eastern spring was rising on its purple wing.

There was a sulphur-hued butterfly flitting across the open window while Flossie read, one of the first of the year's butterflies. The Persian lilacs in front of the house were in bloom, and the hawthorns were in bud. All the air was full of sweet odours, and the warm sunshine comforted the sleeper like a draught of strong wine.

He slept better than he had slept for some days, for his slumbers of late had been fitful and brief. For a little while he could hear Flossie's voice flowing on like a drowsy rivulet deep in the heart of a wood, and then he was verily in dreamland, where there were other voices and other faces.

He was in India again, in the cantonments before Delhi. Yonder above the ridge glittered the tall minarets of the Jumma Musjid, the chief mosque, dominating all lesser and lower buildings from its rocky eminence in the heart of the city.

Old comrades and old friends were round him. The faces of the dying—and how many a brave soldier had perished from sword or sickness in that dreary time of waiting!—looked up at him with the sad farewell smile. Then he fancied himself in the thick of a sudden skirmish before the walls of the city, all hurry and confusion, the black faces of the Pandies grinning through the smoke of their guns, the scarlet turbans and sashes of his own horsemen making spots of colour in the gloom.

Then the smoke rolled away, the golden pinnacles of mosque and palace melted into the blue of an English April sky, daffodils were blowing, blackbirds whistling, and Barbara and he were in the garden hand in hand.

The little hand lay in his. He clasped it, and it had a substance never felt in dreams—a hand that trembled in his, a living hand that tenderly returned his fond pressure.

'Barbara!' he cried; and then he started out of sleep and saw her kneeling beside his bed, pale as a snowdrop, with tearful eyes uplifted to his face.

'Barbara, my love! O, how good, how pitiful of you to come!'

'Did you think I should stay away when I heard that you had asked for me?'

'No, dearest, I thought you would come; I could not sleep last night for the thought of your coming. I lay awake and listened to the ticking of my watch, counting the minutes that must pass before I could see you. And to-day at every sound I fancied you were on the threshold. Yet when you really came I was lying like a log, and knew nothing. How long have you been in the room?'

'Five minutes at the most. I heard you were asleep, and crept softly in to wait for your waking. Even if you had not asked for me, I should have come. I had Vyvyan's leave to come to you. Our journey had been arranged before Flossie's letter came. It was Vyvyan's own idea. He is in the house. He wants to thank you for saving his life. He was not himself that day when you were at Place, and now he feels that he must have seemed ungrateful.'

'I did no more than I would have done for a stranger, Barbara. He owes me no thanks.'

'He and I think otherwise. But for you he might have died, died of poison. It is too horrible to think of. But for you! O, thank God you were near us, thank God you were able to help us!'

'You have a son, Barbara,' said George Leland, after a brief silence. 'Flossie told me.'

'Yes ; he is the dearest creature. Will you see him by and by, if—if—it will not worry you ?'

'It will delight me. I shall feel such joy as Simeon felt. Ah, Barbara, sometimes in my dreams far away I have pictured you with your son lying in your arms, fair as the Mother of God. Idle dreams, foreshadowing happiness that was never to be mine. Sit beside my pillow, love—there, in your sister's chair —so that I can see your face. Such meetings and such partings must come in many lives, I suppose ; but they wrench a man's heartstrings. And yet I saw so much of pain and parting in the East that I fancied I had worn out my capacity for pity, and now I am pitying myself because I must leave the world in which you live.'

' George !'

' Do you remember that morning at Southampton when I saw your sweet pale face at the station ; when you called my name with a little choking cry, and then fell fainting on my shoulder ? Barbara, looking back at that morning I am sorry I did not change the whole plan of my existence, give up every hope of fame and honour, hazard even the stigma of poltroonery, so that I might stay in England and make you my wife. What can life give a man better than happiness, and you and **I might have been** happy ? Yes, love, we might. We should have begun life as paupers ; but I would have found some **way** of winning **our bread, the** hope and energy within me would have made it easy. So happy **a** man must have succeeded. **Barbara, I was a fool to** part from you that morning !'

' Dear George, you know you did what was right. You took the only course possible. Could I have esteemed you had you been so weak as to sacrifice your profession for my sake ?'

' You would have loved me for the love that made me **weak**. No, sweetest, **you** are wise and right.   I could not have sacrificed my calling without sacrificing my honour.   God meant me to be a soldier.   And I did good work yonder; there is comfort in that.   The work done will remain when I am dust.'

He lay back upon his pillow for a little while with closed eyes.   Then came a painful fit of coughing, and Barbara's gentle hand wiped the perspiration from his brow and gave him the lemonade that stood ready on the table by his sofa.

'I should like to see your husband,' he said presently, when he had recovered from the exhaustion that followed the cough.   'I want to thank him for bringing you.'

'He shall come to you this moment.'

She went to the door and called Flossie.   Penruth of Place had been sitting meekly in the neat little kitchen with Mrs. Trevornock; Amelia scrubbing at her pots and pans in the adjacent scullery, and singing, 'Ever of thee I'm faw-aw-awndly dreaming,' in a voice subdued in harmony with the pervading quiet of the house.

'Ask Vyvyan to come, Flossie,' whispered Barbara;

and the Squire came **silently and stood** beside his dying rival's sofa, looking down at him with grave pitying eyes, as a man in the fulness and vigour of strength newly restored might look at fading manhood.

'I am sorry to see you brought so low,' he said, with unusual gentleness.

'Do not be sorry for me. I had very little to live for—except duty. I have had twelve years of that; and perhaps have done harder work in those twelve years than many men **do** in a long life. I don't think my life has been quite useless and purposeless—and—' with a smile—'I have had enough of it. I am glad to go to the land where the wicked cease from troubling, and the weary are at rest.'

'I want to thank you for saving my life. I treated you churlishly that day, for I fancied life was not worth keeping. **But,** God be praised, I have learnt a new lesson since then. I thank you from my soul. But for you I believe I should be lying in my grave.'

'**How** shall I thank you for bringing your wife here to-day?'

'I need no thanks. I brought her as I would have brought her to her brother, for I know that she is pure and true, and I have faith in the man who snatched me from the jaws of death.'

Vyvyan and Barbara left the sick-room after this, and Flossie resumed her accustomed seat near the . sofa. The doctors had said that the invalid was to have plenty of repose. He might have cheerful society, and should be amused as much as possible; but there must be intervals of silence and rest.

'I have some people to call upon in London, Barbara,' said Mr. Penruth, in the hall. 'You can stop with your mother. I'll come back in the evening to take you to the hotel, or you can stay here to-night, if you prefer it.'

She only answered with a loving pressure of the hand he had laid upon her shoulder. She looked at him gratefully, with eyes in which there was pathos too deep for tears ; and so in silence he left her. Mrs. Trevornock was up-stairs with Gilmore and the baby-heir, offering worship to that piece of infantine perfection. The house was very quiet. Barbara looked round her with a vague feeling, as if she had

suddenly found herself there in a dream. Slowly
and gradually the memory of her last morning at
home came back to her, a gray and chilly picture:
the sunless spring morning, the stern-visaged bride-
groom; her mother's trembling hands helping to
arrange her simple bridal attire; all the joylessness
of that day which should have been brimming over
with joy. With what a fond regret she had looked
back at the past, standing on the brink of a new
life! With what shuddering aversion she had shrunk
from every thought of the future!

And now the years had come and gone, not all
unhappy, and she was reconciled to the grim husband
and the lonely home; and there was a new sunshine
that lighted up the dull gray life into beauty, and
filled the future with promise.

'I can never be unhappy while my darling is with
me, and I can never forget my husband's goodness
to-day,' she said to herself.

She looked at the little hall, with its simple
adornments: an engraving after Landseer, the
'Shepherd's Prayer,' a late acquisition of Mrs. Trevornock's; the bowl of wallflowers on the mahogany

slab. How small everything looked, and how ridiculously modern, after the low wide rooms at Place, the sombre panelling, the dusky old pictures, the gleaming armour, and faded arras!

Yet there was a tenderness in her heart for this old home which was almost pain.

'O the happy struggling life,' she thought, ' when a five-pound note was rapture, and a tax-paper despair! Am I the same woman who used to set out with Flossie to buy tea and sugar, and to come back in the gloaming to see the fire burning merrily, as we came round the curve of the lane, and the dusky outline of mother sitting beside the hearth waiting for us?'

There was a little side-door leading into the garden. She went out and walked slowly across the daisy-sprinkled grass, her mind full of memories.

There were the two basket chairs in which she and Flossie had spent so many summer afternoons, reading or working, before George Leland's coming, and where, afterwards, he and Barbara had sat side by side reading Byron, or talking of the future that was to be theirs far away in the shadow of the Himalayas, building castles and planning **a** life of impossible happiness.

She sank into one of the **chairs,** weary with the weight of sadness. He was dying. Flossie had told her what the doctor had said yesterday. **His life was** now only a question of days and hours. **He** might linger for **a week, he might die** before the night. **Nothing more could be done** to prolong the **struggle.** The end was inevitable.

'**So good, so brave, so true !**' she thought; 'and to-morrow there may be no such **man** as George Leland upon this earth—a memory **only, a dear and** cherished name.'

At this thought the tears came. **She** gave herself **up to a** passionate burst of grief; she fell on **her** knees upon the grass, and hid her face upon her folded arms in an attitude **that** looked **like** prayer.

She knew not how long **she had been kneeling** thus **when a hand** lightly touched her shoulder, **and** looking **up** she **saw** George Leland standing **by her** side leaning on his stick.

'Barbara, my love, you must not regret me,' he said **gently.** '**You** do not **know how** happy I am ;

yes, completely happy. To have you here at the last, to know that your husband is stanch and good, and loves you with a worthy love—is not all this enough to make death easy? Do you think I am sorry because I have not been allowed to go on living to feebleness and gray hairs, to be lifted on my horse by a couple of troopers, or to have to ask an aide-de-camp which way my men are facing, because my own old eyes are too blind to see? I have seen veterans commanding armies when it would have been better for themselves and their country they were under the sod. I shall not live to the useless age, Barbara.'

His eye brightened and his hollow cheek flushed as he talked. Looking at him, she began to wonder if the doctors could be right—if there were not too much life and energy here to be the prey of death.

'I am so glad you are well enough to walk in the garden,' she said.

'I struggle for that every day; the air and sunlight and flowers do me more good than doctor's stuff. Dear old garden! Do you remember our moonlight waltzes?'

'I shall never forget them.'

'And the mawkish "Prima Donna"? One of the regimental bands played that unforgotten waltz one day at a review, and at the first bar I felt as if somebody had stabbed me. The melody brought back the old time, and you were resting lightly on my arm as we went slowly round upon the grass. Well, I suppose it is something for a man to be able to say that, for two months of his life, he was utterly happy. Will you come for a stroll round the garden? May I lean upon your shoulder as I do on Flossie's?'

'Pray do.'

They walked slowly along the narrow path by the hazels. This part of the garden was white and rosy with apple-blossoms, and perfumed with wall-flowers. The bright glad sunshine, the happy look of the flowers, tortured Barbara's heart. It was as if there was gladness everywhere, although he was so soon to die.

They came to the corner where the lilies of the valley grew under the fig-tree, whose crinkled leaves were just unfolding.

'How well I remember this spot,' he said, stopping to take breath, 'and your telling me how you buried your canary here, under the lilies! Have you forgotten?'

'No,' she said; 'I buried something here afterwards, something dearer than my canary, though I was foolish enough to be almost heart-broken when he died.'

'Another favourite bird?'

'Your letters. I kept them till my wedding morning, and then I made up my mind to burn them. But I had not the heart to do it. So I came here at daybreak, and dug a grave, dug the grave of my first love. The lilies are growing over your letters, George; the letters that once made me so happy, and the last cruel letter that broke my heart.'

'That cruelty was meant for kindness, Barbara. You can never know the struggle it cost me to write that letter.'

'Well, it changed our fate, that was all. Suppose, instead of doing what you thought your duty, and writing as you did, you had said, "I am in great trouble. Come and be my wife!" I should have gone out to you by the next steamer, just as I went to Southampton.'

'And you would have found me a disgraced man, without a hope of promotion; a pauper, without a chance of fortune; and you would have had good cause to think me the meanest hound in India.'

'I would have trusted you against all the world.'

'Dear love, I was not base enough to profit by such trustfulness; that was why I wrote as I did, vaguely, so that my letter should not be an appeal to your generosity.'

They went slowly along by the wall, and the southern border which pretended to grow strawberries, and succeeded admirably in producing groundsell; groundsell with which Flossie waged an intermittent warfare, and which always got the better of her; for it grew while she was asleep, and waxed strong in her every interval of idleness.

One circuit of the half-acre garden was now as much as George Leland could manage. He was glad to go in and lie down presently, and then Barbara left him to her sister's care.

It was a day full of sadness. Even Mrs. Trevornock's delight in her grandson was damped by her
sorrow for that brave spirit passing away. She and
Flossie took it in turns to sit with the invalid, while
Barbara sat alone in her mother's bedroom with her
baby on her lap. She had made her journey from
the far western point of England to see George
Leland once more; but she submitted quietly to
remain away from him in these last sad hours,
while others tended him and kept him company.
She could not trust herself to watch by him as
Flossie watched; she could not have so schooled her
countenance, so governed her voice. Her sorrow must
have burst from her in some sudden passion which
would have given a new agony to the dying man.

She sat by the open window while the sun went
down behind distant spires and chimneys, and the
evening shadows crept into the room; sat there thinking of the past, and the happy girlish days when she
had stood before yonder looking-glass decking herself
for an evening's pleasure with her betrothed—opera,
or play, or concert—a slender figure, robed in white,
with flowers in her hair, the fond mother waiting

upon her, and hanging about her, and admiring her all the time ; and impatient Flossie standing by imploring to be hooked or pinned, and protesting she should never be ready when the cab came to fetch them ; and then the lover's resonant voice calling at the foot of the little staircase.

And he lay dying in the room where they two had been so happy together, and she was another man's wife !

There was an awful stillness in the house. No one came near her, except Gilmore, who brought her a cup of tea, and made the baby a cosy nest on Mrs. Trevornock's bed.

' Shall I bring candles, ma'am ?' asked Gilmore, when her little charge had been hushed and patted and wheedled to sleep. ' It's so dismal for you sitting up here alone in the dark.'

' No, thank you, Gilmore. I'd rather be as I am.'

So Gilmore curtsied and retired, and Barbara was alone once more.

She had her mother's Testament open before her, the large print clearly visible in the gloaming to eyes familiar with the text :

'I am the resurrection and the life: he that believeth in Me, though he were dead, yet shall he live.'

The moon had risen—a pale young moon—above opening bloom and folded leaf; the evening was wearing on towards night, when Flossie opened the door, and came creeping up to Barbara, her face blotted with tears.

'Come,' she sobbed; 'mother says he is sinking fast. And he would like to see you once more.'

Barbara rose and went without a word.

The garden window was open wide to the soft moonlit sky. There was a shaded lamp near the bed on which George Leland lay; and by the dim light Barbara saw the awful change in his face, the glazing eye, the cold gray hue of the cheek. She knelt by the bed, and he stretched out his hands to her feebly, as if he were groping for something beyond his reach, till one hand rested on her forehead.

'Is this Barbara?'

'Yes.'

' Thank God ! Barbara and England ! I thought
I was in the hospital at Lucknow, and that there
were black faces round my bed.   To die at home ;
to hear your voice at last.   That is happiness.'

Later, awakening from a brief sleep, he murmured, ' Lycurgus decreed that only the Spartans
who had fought for their country were to be buried
in red cloth and olive-leaves, and to have their
names inscribed upon their tombs.   In that rude
age valour was virtue.'   Then, after an interval in
which he lay with half-closed eyes, murmuring
strange snatches of speech, sometimes the name of
a brother officer—Chamberlain, Seaton, Light—
sometimes the word of command to his own men, he
lifted himself suddenly from his pillow, opened his
eyes, looked at Barbara long and earnestly, and then,
extending his wasted arms, drew her to his breast
and kissed her pale lips, murmuring, ' This once,
love, and for the last time.   Dearest, if in a better
world we see and know those whom we have loved
on earth, this is not parting.'

She knelt for a long time by his bed, he lying
sometimes in silence, sometimes with intervals of

wandering speech, sometimes with gleams of consciousness; but through all the feeble hand held
hers, as if there were comfort in her touch. And
thus, at the stroke of midnight, he passed from a
brief interval of troubled sleep to the placid slumber
which knows no earthly waking.

EPILOGUE.

TEN years have come and gone since George Leland was laid in his last rest in the Somersetshire churchyard, where his mother and father had been buried before him. The Indian Mutiny has become history: **Outram, the** Bayard of India, is lying in Westminster Abbey; Clyde, too, is gone, full of years and of honours; Napier is winning new laurels on a strange soil. The world is altered and aged by a decade. Society has grown more artistic, and perhaps more artificial. To the old-fashioned port-and-sherry period has succeeded a milder age of hock **and claret.** Men drink less, women more. **The value of a** sovereign has diminished by thirty per cent. Everybody worth speaking of is rich. **Everybody** worth mention has newly furnished his house, and taken to collecting old china.

But as in the days of the Commonwealth architecture in Cornwall remained still pretty much what **it had been** in the reign of Elizabeth, so now the

old house on the moor is slow to follow the caprices
of London fashion. Everything at Penruth Place
has the same grave and sober air as of old—the
same neutral tints, dull grays, and faded greens pre-
dominate in the furniture, making an admirable
background for the wealth of exquisite flowers with
which Barbara Penruth loves to decorate her rooms.

Yet, though the house is grave and gray as of
old, there is now within its walls all the life and
gladness of a large household and a happy band of
light-hearted children. The ten-year-old heir is not
alone in his nursery; there are two slender blue-
eyed girls, with long fair hair, either of whom might
have sat for Millais' picture of 'My First Sermon.'
There is a toddling boy-baby, unanimously pronounced the very finest thing in babies, an entirely
new development of infantine life, and immeasurably
superior to the infant-heir about whom so much fuss
was made ten years ago. Then there are Mark's
two tall lads from Helstone Grammar-school, and
the eldest son, Jack, home from Oxford for a seemingly interminable vacation which he calls 'the
Long,' a period ostensibly employed in coaching

with a tutor, but the greater **part** of which **is de-**
voted to dogs, horses, and guns. And lastly, there
are two fairy-like girls of seven and five **years,** and
one ridiculously chubby boy aged **two, who also**
claim Mark for father.

Who **is** Mark's second wife and the mother of
these new and tender sprouts upon the family tree
of Penruth? Who **but** this neat little matron, who
rides to hounds in a short olive-green habit and a
tall chimney-pot hat, who is always first in **the**
scurry, and who needs **no** guide to show her **the**
shortest way across country. This fearless rider,
this happy little matron, is Flossie, who, after Mark
had patiently courted her for a period of between
three and four years, during which he bore more
snubbing and ridicule than ever a man endured from
a sharp-tongued mistress, finally relented one day,
as she and Mark were waiting for the hounds in a
sheltered corner beside a copse, and promised **to**
make him unutterably happy for the rest of his life.

She has kept her promise nobly : Mark is as
happy and as true-hearted as he was once false and
miserable. The quarries have prospered with the

growing prosperity of the building trade; and Mark, who is now a partner in the business, has become a rich man. He has built himself a house with a windy bell-tower on the hill outside Launceston, and looks down upon a lower world from brand-new plate-glass windows. Everything in Flossie's house contrasts curiously with the surroundings of her sister. Furniture and ornaments are the essence of newness, and are faintly suggestive of the fancy repository in the Walworth-road. The prismatic hues of much Bohemian glass glorify the drawing-room, where proofs after Landseer stand darkly out against a white-and-gold paper, and upon whose carpet all Flora's gems are represented in their gayest colours. Launceston matrons who have never envied Barbara her grand old Tudor house feel the pangs of the covetous when they behold Mrs. Mark Penruth's plate-glass windows and French china shepherdesses.

And Barbara is happy. Her cup is filled to the brim with domestic joys: the love of little children, who grow dearer to her and fill her life more completely day by day; the love of her proud and happy mother, on whose gentle face the shadows of time fall

so lightly that she is prettier with gray hair than she
was when her dark-brown tresses showed no streak
of silver; the deep affection of a husband who has
won her heart by long years of unchanging fidelity,
unselfish devotion. She has these blessings, and
knows their worth, and is grateful to the God who,
in withholding something, has yet given so much.
And when memory, awakened by a sound, an image,
a vagrant thought, wanders back to the passionate
hopes and dreams of her girlhood, she sees the picture of the past in a tender light which is not all
sorrow and bitterness.

'My hero!' she says to herself sometimes. 'I
am proud to have loved him, and to have been beloved by him; proud to remember how he lived and
how he died.'

He is something in her life still, an ever-abiding
influence; for the dead we have truly loved have
their part in our lives to the end. The memory of
him is interwoven with the very fabric of her mind.
And thus, in the calm afternoon light of a simple
domestic life, loving and beloved, Barbara's story
closes.

Thomas Trevornock, still familiarly described by
Flossie as M. T., has gone to his last earthly rest.
He died not exactly in the odour of sanctity, but at a
most convenient season, and just in time to escape
possible involvement in a criminal prosecution, on
account of certain artful and deeply-laid schemes in
the silver-mining line, which same process brought
Mr. Maulford's ruddy locks under the shears of the
prison barber, and most abruptly put a fullstop, or
at least a colon, in the shape of seven years' penal
servitude, to that clever gentleman's promising career. In vain did Lewis Maulford's counsel enlarge
upon the youthful innocence of his client; in vain
portray, with pathetic eloquence, the affliction of a
widowed mother, harshly deprived of the most devoted and dutiful of sons. A heartless jury found
the prisoner guilty, and an equally heartless judge
pronounced the sternest sentence which the law
allowed. Happily for the honour of the Penruths,
the junior partner had been the active agent in these
fraudulent endeavours to achieve fortune, and Mr.
Trevornock's name was not blazoned in the public
prints, or bandied on the lips of counsel. He may

have been innocent of any knowledge of, or participation in, Lewis Maulford's schemes, although his office had been used by that gentleman as a base of operations.

Miss Penruth has taken up her permanent abode in one of the most commanding terraces that overlook Plymouth Hoe. From that altitude, as from a citadel, she surveys a world which is not worthy of her, and provides tea, toast, and other light refreshments for a select and evangelical few every Tuesday evening at eight.

Mrs. Trevornock still retains the cottage at Camberwell, though the greater part of her life is spent at Place, where her grandchildren adore her, and where she is as dear to her daughter's husband and as popular with the entire household as if the name of mother-in-law had never been made a word of fear.

The Camberwell home is a pleasant shelter for Mark and Flossie when they give themselves a fortnight's holiday in London, and go the round of the West-end theatres. Barbara and her children sometimes visit there, and sit in the old wicker chairs on the lawn, which seems so small to eyes accustomed to the wide lawns and winding shrubbery walks at Place. But it is grandmamma's garden, and, as such, has a certain dignity and distinction in the children's eyes, to say nothing of the greater liberty for mischief which they enjoy here, where there is no stern Scotch gardener to complain of their depredations, or to bewail the havoc they make.

The lilies of the valley bloom and multiply above the spot where Barbara buried her love-letters, and no one knows of the broken story they cover. In every life, even that which seems brightest and fairest, there is some such grave where dead hopes and unfulfilled dreams lie buried.

THE END.

LONDON :

ROBSON AND SONS, PRINTERS, PANCRAS ROAD, N.W

www.ingramcontent.com/pod-product-compliance
Lightning Source LLC
Chambersburg PA
CBHW031345020726
47499CB00005B/1409